I0572157

"Queerbetika - queering rebetika"

Written, researched and compiled by Michael Alexandratos
Translations are all my own unless otherwise noted

First presented at the Museum of Contemporary Art (Sydney)
Zine Fair on Sunday, May 5, 2019

Cycladic Press © 2019
Sydney, Australia

Instagram: @cycladic.press
Inquiries: cycladic.press@gmail.com

ISBN: 978-0-646-89075-3

Cover photo:

Yiannis Papaioannou (1914-1972) dancing *tsifteteli* in drag in the suburb of
Kokkinia, c. 1960s. *Scan courtesy of the Gennadius Library, Athens,
Elias Petropoulos papers.*

Introduction

"Queerbetika" is a term I use to describe the queering of the genre of *rebetika* – an urban Greek popular song from the late 19th century to the 1950s – through academic or creative interventions.

As a scholarly project its broad aim is to research and critically analyse gender and sexuality within and around the genre – including but not limited to its exponents, lyrics, dances, social context and discourses – with a particular focus on "queer" or non-normative genders, sexualities and expressions.

As a creative intervention it can involve literary fiction, art installations, zines, performance, and the "queering" of existing song-texts. This two-pronged attack – both academic and creative – is vital in resisting the "regimes of the normal" that are propagated by researchers and practitioners when they ignore, erase or obscure queer elements of the genre, regardless of how "insignificant" or "marginal" they may be perceived.

It is important to note that my use of this neologism is not intended solely as a slick catchphrase. Many theorists and activists have described the possibilities opened up when we employ the term "queer" as a radical alternative to the LGBTQ (Lesbian, Gay, Bisexual, Transgender, Queer) acronym, in that it allows for people to "recognize, cultivate, and celebrate lives that don't 'line up' with social (heterosexual) norms" and moves away from the alignments associated with terms like lesbian or gay (Kumbier 2014: 5-8).

The possibilities that "queer" enables extends beyond the inquiries of gender and sexuality, and can address intersections like race, ethnicity, nationality, migration and class – all issues which feature prominently in rebetika discourse. Kathleen Dixon writes:

> "There is a great deal more to be said about the complex conjunction of nationality, class, gender, and sexuality in regards to both *rebetiko* and *entechno laiko*--and all of these in relation to the "backward East" and "progressive West" formation." (Dixon, 2018: 12)

Adopting a "queer" approach would therefore seek to challenge commonly-expressed binaries in rebetika discourse, including the East vs. West formation.

Gail Holst-Warhaft noted that while many have observed the split nature of modern Greek identity, that "like all dichotomies, the division is not a clean one." Holst then uses Michael Herzfeld's distinction that "the dichotomy is itself both a European notion and a literate device" which "tends to reinforce stereotypes" about gender, and further about sexuality (2000: 87-88).

It would be useful to list some common binaries evoked in discourses around the rebetika, divisions which are not as clear-cut as they seem:

> East vs. West
> Hellenic vs. Romaic
> urban song vs. rural song
> Asia Minor-style vs. Piraeus-style
> Underworld music vs. not underworld music
> *rebetis* vs. *nikokyris*

Challenging commonly held assumptions around the masculinity (and thus compulsory heterosexuality) of the genre's main protagonists, the low-life macho *rebetes* or *manges* is another task facing the Queerbetika researcher.

That the haunts of these social types were almost exclusively male, including the "hashish dens, the merchant navy, the prisons, and the dockyards" and that the songs and dances of the rebetika flourished within these environments (Holst, 2003: 177) has spurred little commentary or investigation.

Along with Holst, the writings of rebetika scholar Stathis Gauntlett are a good starting point for deconstructing the prodigal rebetis. In a recent essay, Gauntlett again reinforced his view of the performative nature of '*rebetia*' and surmised that being a rebetis is basically about opportunistic posturing, dressing, posing and singing about being tough. These designated roles, Gauntlett stresses, are more "rhetorical constructs... than scientific descriptions of actual people, and they are infinitely variable." (Gauntlett, 2019: 108).

In a 1934 recording of a song entitled "The Rebetis", credited to Kostas Roumeliotis, we are treated to a stereotypical portrait of a character who "hangs around the taverna", "dances to the laterna", "smokes hash without a care" and "keeps his distance from the fag boys".

Ethnographic accuracy was probably not Roumeliotis's intention in drafting lyrics that identified queers within the rebetiko milieu. Rather, his inclusion of the word for "fag" (*digi-dang* – **ντίγκι-ντάνγκ**) might have been simply to rhyme with the word in the preceding line: *merakladang* (**μερακλαντάνγκ**).

Folklorist and rebetika historian Elias Petropoulos (1928-2003) was the first to point out a connection between the world of the rebetes and homosexuality, in the first book-length investigation of the genre, titled "Rebetika Songs: A Folkloric Study":

> "Homosexuality is something well known amongst the rebetes. In prisons, they distinguish the "effeminates" from the "chickens", who do not otherwise engage in homosexual activity, but who sell themselves for cash to prisoners who share the same cell...In the 19th century, songs from the cities were dubbed "queer" (*πούστικα*). However, rebetika songs in particular show total ignorance of effeminates."
> (Petropoulos, 1968: 64)

Although Petropoulos is renowned for his tendencies towards mythopoesis and broad generalisations, the claim that "rebetika songs show total ignorance of effeminates" is actually supported by the evidence – chiefly in the lyrics to the commercially-recorded rebetika, with a few notable exceptions.

There are only three songs that use words denoting a male homosexual: in the song "Toumbeleki, Toumbeleki" (1931), **τιούτο** – (lit. *'one such'*), the aforementioned song by Roumeliotis, and in the comic theatre routine "The Mangas's Lexicon" (1930), both of which use the term **ντίγκι-ντάνγκ** (lit. *ding-dong*). As a contrast, there are at least six songs in the recorded rebetika that make reference to non-gender-conforming women and lesbian sexuality (see anthology).

78rpm record label for "Toumbeleki Toumbeleki". *Courtesy of Tony Klein.*

Petropoulos's claim around "queer" city songs is also intriguing but unverifiable. As rebetika is, more or less, an "urban" genre, that emerged in the late-19th century, could it have a connection or association with the sexual minorities that would have started to congregate in the rapidly expanding urban centres of Greece at that time? Without any other reliable sources to draw from, it is difficult to answer that question with any certainty.

However, we do know that amongst the exponents of rebetika, there are at least two whom we can confidently reclaim as "queer": the "lesbian icon" Sotiria Bellou (1921-1997) and the queer refugee crooner Kostas Nouros (1892-1972).

I defend my use of hearsay in this text by the very fact that it records information about exponents that would otherwise remain undocumented and uncontested. Regardless of whether they lead to any definitive insights or "truths" into the actual sexual and gender expressions of exponents, they are valuable for revealing what Kostas Yannakopoulos calls the "truth of unveiling" or the "gendered/sexual imaginary" (2016: 174).

The taboos surrounding homosexuality in Greece have severely hampered any discussion or investigation into how this aspect of identity has informed the genre, in all of its facets.

When I was in Athens in late-2018, I phoned renowned record collector and researcher Panayotis Kounadis to inquire about my research. In short, he was totally flabbergasted by the suggestion that this topic could be related in any way to rebetiko. When I pointed to the fact that both Nouros and Bellou were gay he became even more defensive, telling me that there was no such thing, and expressed disbelief at how or where I came across such an idea. Curiously, in the liner notes to a CD reissue of Nouros's recordings, Kounadis completely erases Nouros's queerness and makes no mention of his homosexuality.

Looking for other outlets of queer expression, we can identify the *tsifteteli* (a kind of belly dance) as one that even allowed "straight" men to experiment with gender roles. Although its association with femininity meant that it was mainly danced by women and queer men, Holst observed that in 1960s Athens, married men would dance it it together while holding their testicles and imitating the movements of female dancers. Holst writes that:

> "This playful gender reversal in the dance should not be read,
> necessarily, as indicative of a homoerotic relationship between
> the dancers...Sometimes a participant would bring along
> a wig to make the spectacle more amusing. The shouting about
> homosexuality and the ribald laughter continued until the men
> tired and went home to their wives." (Holst, 2003: 177)

Holst concludes this passage with an important point, that "undoubtedly homosexual activity existed in rebetika circles, but...it was neither the norm nor the ideal." (2003: 177)

***

I have inevitably taken a scattershot approach in writing and compiling this zine. However, through its structure I have outlined three broad areas of inquiry that can be taken up by future researchers or creative practitioners: into **exponents**, **sites of performance** and **discourses** produced by gay, pro-rebetika intellectuals and artists.

I stress that this publication is not meant to be a definitive look into queerness and homosexuality within the genre. I raise many ideas and arguments that need to be fleshed out further. A thoroughly academic approach is not one that I've adopted, nor have I incorporated much critical theory and analysis. This is a task I could undertake more seriously through academic research.

Instead, this zine serves as a cursory attempt to collect information that has not been published before in one place, and to frame it using a "queer" lens.

***

Vassilis Tsitsanis (1915-1984), the king of post-war rebetiko and *laiko*, wrote lyrics to a song whose sentiments we can re-imagine as one of acceptance for all the peripheral people of rebetiko, including refugees, the working class, drug addicts, sex workers and queers:

> Come as you are, come as you are,
> Don't ruin my fun and dampen my fire!
>
> The night is ours, the night is ours
> And we must party with all of our soul.

It is a good sentiment as any to conclude this introduction. Meanwhile, the battle continues…

Michael Alexandratos,
Sydney, April 15, 2019.

1. Exponents

Left to right: Nikos Syrigos (violin), Michalis Skouloudis (mandolin), Giorgos Petridis (cimbalom), Kostas Nouros (singer), Stellakis Perpiniadis (guitar). Dated to 1928. *Courtesy of the Gennadius Library, Elias Petropoulos papers.*

Kostas Nouros (and the queer amane)

Kostas Nouros (1892-1972) is the only exponent active during the inter-war era of rebetiko whom we can confidently reclaim as "gay" or "queer." Part of a generation of singers and musicians who migrated to Greece following the Asia Minor Catastrophe of 1922, Nouros excelled in his recorded performances of _amanedes_, (vocal improvisations based on Ottoman musical "modes"), as well as traditional and popular songs that fall under the generic category of rebetiko song.

Born in Smyrna, or present-day Izmir, Turkey, in 1892 as Konstantinos Masselos, he became better known under the pseudonym "Nouros", a word derived from Kurdish, meaning "fire." His family emigrated to Smyrna while he was still an infant, and at age two he was orphaned of his mother. Nouros's father never remarried, so he was brought up by a lady neighbour who tended to a cemetery opposite their home. As a child he took a great interest in Greek Orthodox chanting and sang with the cantors at local churches in Smyrna.

According to Panayotis Kounadis (1993), it was after Nouros turned 18 that he travelled to Mount Athos to become a monk. What transpired next must have been pivotal for the young Nouros, as he apparently stayed on Mount Athos for only a few days before returning home to Smyrna. It is tantalising to speculate on the events that took place, or on the thoughts in young Nouros's mind that lead to this decision. The burgeoning awareness of his own sexuality, his difference, could have played a role in this situation. Alternatively, his decision to enter monastic life could have been formulated for purely pragmatic reasons.

The years between 1911 to 1922 were turbulent for Nouros. Although he established his career as a singer during this time, he lived through the death of his first wife and had to flee Smyrna as a refugee in the events leading up to the explusion of Greeks from Asia Minor. From 1926-1934 he sang on over 75 recordings which were issued on 78rpm shellac gramophone records. In 1937, the daughter of his second wife, and his only child, died at age seventeen.

With the onset of WWII, he joined the Greek army as an entertainer and escaped the German occupation of Greece by travelling to the Middle East.

By 1946, Nouros was back in Greece, and would continue to perform in various musical venues in Piraeus up until 1962, when he decided to stop singing and live off a meagre pension. He lived out his final years in an impoverished home at 33 Grevenon street, in old Kokkinia. Stathis Gauntlett remembers visiting Nouros in a squalid old age home in Kallithea a few weeks before he died. He was in much pain, and presumably passed away at that same institution on May 26th, 1972.

Photo of 33 Grevenon, Kokkinia, taken in 1972 by journalist Kosta Voulgari a week before Nouros died. *Courtesy of the Gennadius Library, Elias Petropoulos papers.*

Nouros's Sexuality

It is interesting to note that amongst the photographs Petropoulos collected from Nouros, that there were no photos of his first or second wife, and none of his long-dead daughter.

That Nouros's photos were not published in the first edition of Petropoulos's "Rebetika Songs" (1968) suggests that they were collected sometime during the years 1968-1972. Then over 75 years old, it can be assumed that Nouros was willing to part with his personal photographs, or at least allowed Petropoulos to borrow them.

It is unclear whether the iconic photograph of a young Nouros in an ensemble with fellow musicians, dated to 1928, was collected from either Nouros or Stellakis Perpiniadis (1899-1977), who is also pictured in the photo.

Regardless of their exact provenance, 10 out of the 12 surviving photos of Nouros depict him either alone or in the company of younger men. Together they paint a portrait of Nouros as melancholy, mysterious and withdrawn, images that correspond poignantly to the voice heard on his recordings; one leaden with pain and pathos.

Drawing on Kathleen Dixon's research on Sotiria Bellou, and quoting from Sara Ahmed's work, Nouros can quite easily be put into the category of "feminist killjoys, unhappy queers, and melancholic migrants whose refusal to reproduce the family line is seen as the cause of unhappiness." (2018: 4)

One photo of Nouros as an "unhappy queer", was taken in an Athens portrait studio in 1938. Nouros is seated and appears solemn and reserved. To his left a young man, presumably a lover and no older than 20, stands upright with his left hand resting on Nouros's shoulder, the other hidden inside a jacket pocket.

A second photo, apparently taken in Istanbul in 1950, depicts Nouros walking alongside a much younger Turkish aircraftman. His black sunglasses shield his eyes, with a cigarette poised over his mouth.

Nouros the "unhappy queer" with his younger lover, taken in Athens, 1938. *Courtesy of the Gennadius Library, Elias Petropoulos papers.*

"I fall for every step you take and run to chase your shadow..."

Nouros with a younger Turkish aircraftman, taken in Istanbul, 1950.
Courtesy of the Gennadius Library, Elias Petropoulos papers.

The third photo of Nouros pictured with a younger man was first published in an article by Panos Savopoulos, in the periodical Odos Panos, in 2008. The photo comes from the granddaughter of Dimitris Vlahos, whose exact relationship with Nouros is currently unclear.

A resident's permit preserved in the Petropoulos rebetika archive, dated to 11-5-1949, lists Nouros, then 57, living with the 39-year-old Vlahos and his 15-year-old son Kyriakos at his home in Nikaias (old Kokkina). Dimitris Vlahos's occupation is listed as "farmer", while his son is listed as "student."

Nouros's preferences become even more apparent in the following two anecdotes. Read, for example, this dialogue between Kostas Ladopoulos and a close friend of his who grew up in Kokkinia. The respondent first encountered Nouros in 1953, when he was 61 years old, and often saw him seated at an Athletics Club coffeehouse in the company of younger men. Ladopoulos posted this exchange on his blog on June 15, 2008:

> Q: You told me once that you had met Nouros. How old were you then? Did you know who he was? Had you seen a photo of him before?
>
> A: Yes. I had a photo of him from my father who admired him a lot. I saw him at the coffee house of the philathletes at the Athletic Association of Nikaias, which was run by Makis Papadopoulos. The coffee house was found in Agios Nikolaos. I did delivery work…used to sit there too. I saw him there many times. I was around 17-18 years old, mature though and newly initiated into rebetiko.
>
> Q: Do you remember seeing him sitting with others or off to the side?
>
> A: Every time I saw him, he sat off to the side. But not by himself. He usually sat with one or two people who were a lot younger than him in age. He was thin, looked very serious, very masculine. We knew however…

Left: Nouros c. 1940. *Courtesy Gennadius Library.*

Right: Nouros with Dimitris Vlahos (left). Late 1930s?
From the archive of Vlahos' grandaughter Evangelia.

Nouros back in Piraeus, Greece following the end of German occupation, taken 1946. *Courtesy of the Gennadius Library, Elias Petropoulos papers.*

Q: Can you remember if there were any rumours circulating about him?

A: No, there weren't. I would have understood it and heard about it. It was not the case that Nouros was teased or made fun of because of this. He commanded respect wherever he went. He worked and sang at "Kefallas" then, close to the present-day town hall of Nikaias, at the "Gefiraki" that's there now and across from Perivola's *magazi*.

Q: If I asked you, from the few things you've said…when he sat with the young men, can you remember if he gave the impression of a jocular or reserved kind of person?

A: It's hard to say. I remember a person who sat quietly and talked in a low voice. It wasn't just one or two times that I saw him, it was a great deal. I remember a well-dressed person, with a well-kept appearance, serious. And from what you've shown me of his photographs I remember even now. A withdrawn look, serious and melancholic…And like I've told you, Nouros sang even then. He must have made money from it too. He still kept dyeing his hair…Ah, I remember him once when he got up and left, and I looked at the way he walked. Eh, something was up…"

The second anecdote I collected on September 24, 2018 from Athens-based musician and record collector Christos Fanaritis.

In the 1990s, Fanaritis played in an ensemble with a piano player named Sotiris. Fanaritis subsequently invited Sotiris to his home, who wanted to hear gramophone records from his collection. When Fanaritis played him recordings featuring the singing of Nouros, Sotiris said that he had met him while working in the *laika magazia* during the early 1960s in Kokkinia. At the time, Nouros was in his late 60s and had no other source of income, save for the performances he gave at local venues, most notably with the entourage of Vaggelis Perpiniadis Jr (1927-2003).

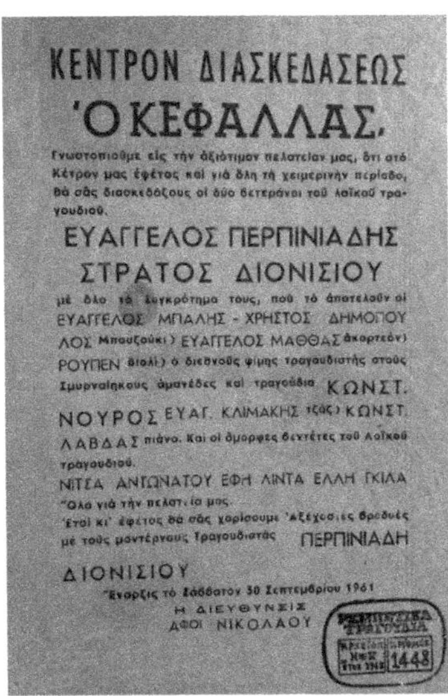

A flyer for the venue "Kefallas" where Nouros sang on 30 September, 1961.

Nouros c. late-1950s.

Nouros (top-right corner) in the ensemble of Perpiniadis Jr, 1959.
Images courtesy of Genadius Library.

One night, Sotiris played piano in an ensemble while Nouros sang his amanedes. Nouros instructed the younger musician to play the piano like a cimbalom, imitating the hard staccato-attack of the hammer. The performance started and Sotiris was hidden in darkness behind the other musicians, when Nouros moved his hand across Sotiris's lap and grabbed his crotch. According to Fanaritis, Sotiris was around 18 years old and didn't protest at his harassment because Nouros was well-respected, and still held some power and prestige at that time.

Stathis Gauntlett also informed me via email correspondence (10/12/2018) that a musician told him how he had been "repeatedly propositioned by Nouros during a collaboration and that this had stopped only when he threatened to beat the latter's lights out."

Ρεμπέτικο | Κείμενο Μελπομένη Μαραγκίδου   08 June 2017, 3:00pm

Η Ζωή και το Έργο του Ρεμπέτη Κώστα Νούρου, που Γούσταρε Γυναίκες και Άνδρες

Η βιογραφία «Κώστας Νούρος: Ξένος, δυο φορές», μιλάει για έναν άνθρωπο που παραλίγο να περάσει στη λήθη.

Nouros's sexuality has been more recently acknowledged in a Greek Vice article regarding a musical production about his life, entitled "Kostas Nouros: Twice a Stranger." (Maragidou, 2017). He is reclaimed in that article not simply as a homosexual, but as a "rebetis" who "was into women and men."

Further, the writer claims that "for his time, it was almost unthinkable for him to be accepted as a rebetis in his chosen occupation with such a different sexual orientation" concluding that "Nouros broke the mould of the typical 'macho' rebetis."

But how accurate is it for us to label him as retrospectively "gay" or "bisexual", both words that are in popular use amongst Anglophone speakers today and which may not be appropriate for Nouros's time and place.

When asked about Nouros's sexuality. the director of "Twice a Stranger" responded with the following:

> "Gossip, gossip, gossip, Anthi…" Mr. Napoleon tells me, a retired teacher who still lives on Grevenon street [where Nouros lived out his final years]: "I remember him, he lived across from us and my mother told me how he was a "*didis*" (**ντιντής**). He always pierced and deflated our soccer balls when they fell in his yard." The word "didis" would even be used by Natasha from the choir, when I told her about my ideas for the production: "My father listened to him a lot, he loved him, however he also told me how he was a didis."

Referring to Nouros, Angela Papazoglou tells Tasos Schorelis in his rebetika anthology that Nouros "was a good kid, despite his 'vice' (**ελάττωμά**)"

Gauntlett also informed me (22/1/2019) that when a friend of his, "an old bouzouki veteran", was asked in 1972 if he'd heard that Nouros was dead, he said among other things: «Ήτανε μάλλον **μπινές** — δηλαδή ούτε για **πούστης** δεν έκανε» (He was surely **bisexual** – that is, he wasn't really a **faggot**). (See glossary - **ντιντής** and **μπινές**).

We can reasonably deduce from all of these anecdotes that Nouros was well-respected and was not derided openly for his sexuality or branded as a *poustis*, a word easily evoked in vernacular Greek. Poustis can be translated as "faggot" and is strongly associated with effeminacy and being the passive sexual partner, traits that conflict with recorded impressions of Nouros as "serious" and "masculine."

The "Queer" Amane

"The *amanes* became emblematic of a style of music that was both admired for its emotional intensity and rejected for its association with the oriental and feminine side of the modern Greek psyche." (Holst, 2000)

I would go further than Holst and argue that the *amanedes* have an implicit association with homosexuality and queerness, along with the "oriental" and "feminine" qualities that are ascribed to it in many debates recorded in newspapers of the 19th and early 20th centuries (see Vlisidis' **Σπάνια Κείμενα**, 2018).

That this style of music was officially banned by both the Greek and Turkish governments in the 1930s, under their respective leaders Ioannis Metaxas (1871-1941) and Kemal Ataturk (1881-1938), is indicative of a rampant nationalist project that sought to banish the spectre of the "Orient" and align both populaces closer to the normative values of procreation and the family unit.

Anna Apostolidou writes that in contemporary public discourse in Greece, gay male sexuality is often referred to as "Ottoman-style" (*othomaniko*), and that the connotations of this term "have been handed down to contemporary Greeks as among the darkest of collective agonies recalling national subordination and mark the disavowal of Ottoman history and, at the same time, the collateral disavowal of local same-sex history and desire." (2017: 71)

Surely, some of the "collective agonies" of the Ottoman yoke as it relates to music and same-sex desire are illustrated in the case of the dancing *yamakia* (also Köçek), who were pre-pubescent boys recruited from the ranks of the non-Muslim subjects (*dhimmi*), including Greeks, Armenians and Jews; a practice phased out in the mid-to-late 19th century.

Roderick Conway Morris writes in his article on Greek Café Music (1981: 71-72):

> "Foreign travellers and residents in the Near East provide many descriptions of the music and dancing boys in the taverns and cafes of Asia Minor and Istanbul, often drawing attention to the dominant role played by Greek performers. As François Charles Pouqueville, for example, writes:
>
>> In the taverns, of which there are an infinite number in the capital of the true believers, there are commonly a sort of dancers called *yamakis*. They are Greeks from the islands of the archipelago, elegantly dressed, with bracelets and necklaces of precious stones, and with very rich shawls. They have long flowing hair, are perfumed with essences, and highly rouged. The indolent Turks are extremely fond of these dancers: they encourage them by large presents of money: and each fixing upon a favourite, they will often finish even by fighting to maintain the superiority of such and such a *yamak*i..."
>
> *(François Charles Pouqueville, 1813, Travels in the Morea, Albania and Other Parts of the Ottoman Empire).*

A köçek dancer in the Ottoman Empire, 19th-century.

At least one commentator has noticed that some of the lyrics to Nouros's amanedes exhibit a queer sensibility. "Sandouri Dean Bey", writes in a post published to his blog Aman Yala in 2006:

> "Regardless of his sexuality, however, the lyrics to some of Nouros' αμανέδες have a decidedly queer sensibility and resonate with my queer ears. Two in particular, **Χουζάμ Μανές** (hou-ZAM ma-NESS) or Ποιός έχει μάυρη την καρδιά, "Whoever has blackness in his heart," and **Χετζάζ Μανές** (he-TZAZ ma-NESS) or Ο κόσμος με κατηγορεί, "The world condemns me"— both recorded in the early 1930s—evoke that sense of "the love that dare not speak its name."

> Χουζάμ Μανές

> Ποιός έχει μάυρη την καρδιά, νά γίνουμε συντρόφοι νά περπατάμε σ'ερημιές νά μη θωρούμε ανθρώποι.

> Whoever has a blackened heart, let's stay together and wander the wastelands and hide ourselves from the world's gaze.

> Χετζάζ Μανές

> Ο κόσμος με κατηγορεί, δίχως νά ξέυρει λέει— αν ήξευρε τον πόνο μου μαζί μου θε νά κλαίει.

> The world condemns me without knowing me—
> if they knew my pain, together they would cry with me

> If Nouros were a homosexual, these lyrics would have had a special poignancy for him. Whether or not he actually loved other men, his αμανέδες speak to contemporary queers (at least those of us listening to Rembetika) about our experience of being marginalized and condemned because of whom we love."

According to the discography of Maniatis, Nouros recorded 36 amanedes, making up almost half of his recorded output. A queer reading of all the song-texts Nouros performed on record is yet to be done.

Markos Vamvakaris – "Saint Macho"

The iconic rebetika singer and bouzouki player Markos Vamvakaris (1905-1972) is one exponent whose masculinity (and thus heterosexuality) has long been unchallenged, no part due to the mythology and idolatry that surrounds his life and work, which has seen him relegated to near-sainthood «ο Άγιος Μάγκας».

Markos: "Saint Macho"

Front cover of Vamvakaris's autobiography, compiled and edited by Angeliki Vellou Kail from Markos's handwritten notes and interviews conducted by Nearchos Georgiadis and Angeliki Kalamara between 1965-1967, as well as supplementary interviews with Keil in 1969. First appeared in 1973 and finally published in Athens in 1978. (Koglin, 2016: 58-59)

However, from Markos's autobiography we learn that he had a soft-spot for animals and flowers. And as a 10-year-old newspaper boy on the island of Syros, his initiation into the seedy urban underworld in the port of Ermoupoli did not only involve exposure to criminals, smuggling, gambling, prostitution and violence - but also homosexuality. Markos recounts in his autobiography that:

"A journalist and publisher called Zoula had a local newspaper *Parartima* and he was looking for young boys to sell his papers. I lost no time, I went to find him and the minute he saw me he took me on. That's how I started on my new 'profession' as a newspaper boy. There were about thirty other kids all selling papers like I was. Our publisher dressed us all in uniform and he provided food and a place to sleep for whoever wanted it. I slept there most nights with the other boys, all together in one room like a barracks and in there you'd see and hear all kinds of things you'd never have imagined!

My mother understood this business wasn't going to do me any good, and she scolded me every day, telling me not to go on with it and above all not to sleep every night with this seedy bunch of boys. I didn't take her seriously because this kind of life had begun to draw me in and with hindsight you could say I was kind of cut out for it. So I went with this work for about two months – long enough to give me a big head and start me on the path I'd be chained to for most of my life. I began to see and get to know close up the rackety life, the underworld, shady dealings, cards and all the crap fate deals out. Not that I took part in it. I was too young. It was risky for a young boy not being at home but in a place where there were smaller boys and bigger ones together. What was I doing there! Bad stuff, bad folk. All kinds of... begging your pardon but they were buggering each other. Some of them went right off the rails later. I mean this place was a bordello. That didn't bother Zoula.

What did he care? These people were looking at money and they made lots of it. All the big-time crooks gathered at Zoula's. Plenty of times the police came and seized one or other of them.

'Hey you filthy faggot! What were you up to yesterday?
Were you stealing from so-and-so?' Beatings, bad goings on I
tell you. I ate my daily dose of *manghia* – by the ladleful!"
(Vamvakaris, 2015: 37-38). *Translated by Noonie Minogue.*

It is not quite clear in this passage if Markos participated in the sexual
ruckus at the boys' barracks, although he definitely witnessed it.

Markos provides another intriguing anecdote featuring an encounter with
a 60-year-old mechanic:

"Ah, what I've been through on the street! Being a bootblack,
being just a lad and a good-looking one too, there were some
vicious types. It's not all good folks in the world. There are bad
guys too. When I was selling papers I used to go to a factory,
Pousialos. It's still there in Syros. There was a mechanic in that
place and he was a right scumbag. Whenever I went there, he
used to grab my cheeks and my bum. *Now this was one
of those things I'd seen and I knew about.* It got to the point
where I said to him one day, 'Hey you, what can I say! I'm going
to serve you up such a feast you'll be shitting yourself!' I didn't
mince my words. 'You think you can do me over you old sod!
You won't know what hit you pal! I'll trash you, you old mother-
fucker, and everybody round here'll be onto you! So many girls,
so many chicks in here. What d'you want with me!'

I didn't want that sort of thing. I steered well clear. I set him
up, this guy, he got thrashed. In the places where I hung about
in the evening, selling papers, I was on good terms with the
boys on the block. They all knew me. It was my patch. One
day I was talking with one of them, a *koutsavakis* type, you
know… 'Look, he's bothering me,' says I, 'How can we fix things
and give him a hiding?' Three guys turned up and they said
'Say you'll meet him at noon in such and such a place.' So that's
what I did. What could he do the poor bugger? The other guys
set about him and give him the mother of all beatings, smashed
him to a pulp. Poor bastard didn't lodge a complaint. What could
he say? I started going to the factory again since there were

other guys there who wanted newspapers. When he came back, 'Hell, Frango!' he says to me – he called me Frango because I was a Catholic and he was Orthodox. 'Hell, Frango, I'd never have believed it…' 'There's plenty more where that came from,' says I to him, 'if you dare speak to me again. If I knew you had a son like me, I'd go and fuck him.' **He was old that guy, fifty-five to sixty years old, a mechanic, sub-mechanic of the factory. He was "that" kind of person.* I** was twelve or thirteen years old then but very tough. And what didn't happen to me! It's a whole heap of things, my life story." (Vamvakaris, 2015: 44-45). *Translated by Noonie Minogue.*

Note Markos's threat to the mechanic, in Greek: «Αν ήξερα ρε, του λέω, πως έχεις γιό σαν και μένα, θα πήγαινα το γιό σου να τον εγαμούσα, του λέω»

Markos seems to be saying" "If I knew you had a son like me [i.e. around my age], I'd go and fuck him [as revenge for what you did to me]." Even in Greek I'd argue that this is an unusual thing to say in this context and could hint at a latent homosexuality. The aggression and dominance involved in being the penetrative or "active" partner in homosex is implicitly stated in this verbal threat. Even if Markos was to engage in such behaviour, he would not be wholly stigmatised as a result of how sexual identity was conceptualised at the time. Using the 1950s-70s as his focus of study, Yannakopoulos writes that:

"In Greek society…the sexual behavior and identity of a man – but also of a woman – was conceptualised based on the gender with which he or she identified, and not on the sexual partner of choice. More specifically, men were not broadly categorized as 'heterosexual' and 'homosexual' but as 'masculine' and 'feminine' (*andras* i.e. man – *poustis adelfi*). A 'masculine' man could have sexual relations with either a 'feminine' man or woman without being stigmatized." (2016: 175)

***This sentence was not translated into English by Noonie Minogue in the 2015 edition of Markos' autobiography. The reasons for this are unknown.**

Markos at home sitting on the staircase that led down to the basement where he worked. *Photo by Nearchos Georgiadis, 1967.*

Further on the subject of pederastic practices, Petropoulos's writings suggest that they existed and persisted in urban areas of Greece in the 19th to mid-20th centuries, particularly amongst the trades. In "Underworld and Shadow Theatre", Petropoulos explains:

> "In Greece, pederasts despise passive homosexuals (*poustidhes*). Nor do the latter ever mix with pederasts. Pederasts hunt handsome boys who, themselves, are not necessarily passive homosexuals. In Greece, there used to exist trades typically composed of pederasts: boatmen, shoemakers, and dealers of small wares were often pederasts, for example...In his text "Paidos! Paidos!" (1940), Menelaos Loudemis describes a group of bricklayers, at least one of whom sodomizes a young Gypsy boy."
> (Petropoulos, 1980: 83-85). *Translated by John Taylor.*

Ed Emery, also records another of Petropoulos's observations of these practices in the fruit and vegetable markets of Athens, where "the people who keep track of writing down the orders are always handsome young boys – the wholesaler's "sultana" [his younger lover]." (2000: 87)

Yiannis Zaimakis, in his book on non-commercial rebetiko, cultural creation and social identity in the disreputable urban district of Lakkos in Heraklion, Crete, writes in a footnote:

> One point which is shrouded in darkness is that of homosexuality. Certain informants [whom he interviewed for his research] avoided the subject when asked for further clarification. Here I mention some characteristic phrases: "in Lakkos there were *kolobarades* too", "there were a few well-known people in the area who had intimate relations with young boys, bum-pinching and the like." (1999: 42)

A *kolobaras* (**κολομπαράς**) can mean a male who is an active homosexual, i.e. a "top", or a pederast who favours young boys or men, and who takes on the role of the masculine *erastis*, again, an "active", penetrative role.

Another point that is "shrouded in darkness" as it relates to rebetika is that of the "queer-mangas", or *poustomangas* [πουστόμαγκας]. As far as we know, the first mention of this word in print is in Petropoulos's dictionary of Greek gay slang, the "Kaliarda", where it is defined as follows:

> **πουστόμαγκας**, o. the tough 'passive' gay (*kinaidos*). A combination of the well-known words *poustis* + *mangas*. Note that the passive gays don't use the word "poustis" and its derivatives (see notes). (1971: 127)

In the 1980 edition of the dictionary, Petropoulos elaborates on this figure in the addenda, writing that:

> "It is high time that I mention one special category of homosexual – referred to as the *poustomangas* – a topic that has long been shrouded in darkness. The poustomangas was himself a 'passive' homosexual, although he was at the same time highly aggressive and belligerent. The poustomangas didn't behave effeminately, he hung around the tough guys (*manges*), and whenever necessary started knife fights. You'd need to have a lot of courage to swear at a poustomangas. The poustomangas associated mostly with the underworld, rather than the queers. And I need to repeat again: male queers can't enter into the caste of the manges.
>
> In Metaxourgeio [a suburb in Athens], before the Second World War, there lived a few well-known *poustomanges*. In my book "Rebetika Songs" I published one photo of Mitsias. Mitsias was the most well-known poustomangas in Thessaloniki. It seems that the infamous Manolia was also a poustomangas. I don't know any other names of people who were poustomanges." (Petropoulos, 1980: 247-248)

Petropoulos claimed in other published works that "women and queers" weren't allowed into the homosocial hang-outs of the manges, including the taverns and the hash-dens, a claim I'd take with caution. The two exceptions to this rule that he notes are the *rebetisses* (female *rebetes*) and the poustomanges. (2000: 62)

Based on his research and interviews with the old inhabitants of Lakkos, Zaimakis drew up a table listing the qualities of those considered "authentic" manges, and those who were "fake" or pseudo-manges.

ΓΝΗΣΙΟΣ ΜΑΓΚΑΣ		ΨΕΥΤΟΜΑΓΚΑΣ	
ΣΥΜΒΟΛΙΚΕΣ ΟΝΟΜΑΣΙΕΣ	ΠΡΟΣΔΙΟΡΙΣΤΙΚΑ ΧΑΡΑΚΤΗΡΙΣΤΙΚΑ	ΣΥΜΒΟΛΙΚΕΣ ΟΝΟΜΑΣΙΕΣ	ΠΡΟΣΔΙΟΡΙΣΤΙΚΑ ΧΑΡΑΚΤΗΡΙΣΤΙΚΑ
ρεμπέτης	ωραίος σωστός εντάξει στο φέρσιμό του	παρδό-μαγκας κωλό-μαγκας	σκάρτος επιδειξίας κάνει φασαρίες
ντερβίσης	μετρημένος στα λόγια δεν ανέχεται να τον προσβάλεις	κουραδό-μαγκας	μιλάει πολύ
μόρτης	σωστός στη παρέα μυαλωμένος	πουστό-μαγκας πουφ-μάγκας μαχαλό-μαγκας	άνθρωπος της μανούβρας
αλάνης	φίνος χασικλής δυνατός άντρας σοβαρός	καροϊδό-μαγκας τσιχλί-μαγκας	ψευτονταής βγάζει σκάρτες

Zaimakis explains:

> In the above table we lay out the certain categories of people from the world of the *manges*, where *rebetis*, *dervisis*, *mortis* and *alanis* are viewed as authentic expressions of the identity of the mangas. On the opposite side are prefixes with negative symbolic content using obscene and profane phrases in the *mangiko* argot for the attribution of special names. Words, such as *"pouf-"*, *"skato-"*, *"pordo-"* concern the dirty and the unclean, and others, such as *"pousto-"*, *"kolo-"* refer to anal penetration and effeminacy, and their invocation was a metaphorical way of rejecting attitudes and behaviours which didn't fit the standards of virile masculinity. (1999: 199-200)

A keepsake photo featuring Mitsias (centre-back) the most well-known "queer-mangas" from Thessaloniki, taken on 12-4-1936 in a prison for youths. Sitting in front of Mitsias is the young Christos Migos, a popular composer and bouzouki player also from Thessaloniki. *Courtesy of the Gennadius Library, Elias Petropoulos papers.*

Design for Petropoulos's dictionary of Greek gay slang, the 'Kaliarda", first published in 1971.

Markos's willingness to even mention the topic of homosexuality is interesting. Based on the following two passages from his autobiography, he seems to have been cognizant of homosexual activity amongst the new generation of bouzouki players active in the 1960s. These behaviours stand in contrast to the old ways of *mangia*, or manliness, toughness, thriftiness and honour. According to Markos, the new players have sold themselves out for money and would do anything to achieve success and recognition, even be fucked! Markos refers to the old vanguard of bouzouki-player rebetes:

> "They weren't money grubbers. Not like these famous guys we have now, the new *bouzoukia*, up to their eyeballs in money. They've gone crazy for it. Nothing else interests them. They've raked it in and they've made it big. Really, they do any kind of shit, even get buggered just to get a taste of the sweet stuff. I'm not saying everyone does this kind of thing, but broadly speaking, I mean, they're degenerates. That's not how it should be. The bouzouki, like I told you, is what the hardened criminals laid hold of." (Vamvakaris, 2015: 113-114). *Trans. Noonie Minogue.*

Markos later quotes another example of the "degeneracy" amongst new players in this short exchange:

> "I know one guy – let's not mention any names – they say to him, 'You're getting fucked.'
> 'I am', says he, 'and I'm proud of it.'
> 'Dammit you old faggot, you fat arse you're getting fucked!'
> 'Proud of it mister.' That's what he replies."
> (Vamvakaris, 2015: 228). *Trans. Noonie Minogue.*

Petropoulos seems to have been cognizant of the goings-on in bouzoukia circles too, writing in the introduction to his book on the underworld that:

> "I record in my book 'Holy Hashish' all that is publishable. That is because I can't, under threat of legal action, talk about how many and which bouzouki players were gay sodomisers, bisexual, hash-heads or wanted criminals." (1991: 11)

A researcher-friend in Athens passed on a rumour that the poet Dinos Christianopoulos had information on Markos's supposedly gay relations with men. My attempts to get into contact with Christianopoulos to clarify this rumour and ask him questions about rebetika were unsuccessful, as he is currently very ill.

More compelling are the two songs credited under Markos's name that express the narrator's love and adoration for a butcher. From 18 to 35 years old Markos worked as a butcher in the slaughterhouses of Athens and Piraeus. In his autobiography, Markos says the following about the subject matter of his songwriting:

> "From 1936-39, I was writing all the time – I was on a roll…I was writing all about girls, you know, love songs. What else would I write about since I was a kid? I have written some others but even those in the end all come back down to love affairs. I've written some about jobs people do." (Vamvakaris, 2015: 265)

He then recites the first verse from his song "The Butcher" which he recorded and sang in 1934. Selected verses below:

> Oh, my butcher with the apron you tie up behind
> Every time I see you my butcher, I go crazy.

> Your knives sparkle, your sharpener shines too
> Your dark eyes shine my fine butcher lad.

Concluding with the verse:

> I love you, my butcher, with your manly ways.
> My butcher I love you, with your manly ways.

Following this song, Markos recites the lyrics to another butcher-inspired ditty, "In The Meat Market", recorded in 1947 and performed by the vocalist Stella Haskil (1918 – 1954). Some chief verses listed below:

> The butcher's boy in the marketplace
> With the bushy brows and the mole on his face.

He's tall and strong and manly, like a lamp he's all ablaze.
You have to know, mama, that I can't help but love him madly.

Markos's song "The Monk" [Ο Καλόγερος], recorded in 1946, can also be interpreted as a desire for him to live in the exclusive company of men after all of his troubles with women. He sings:

I'm fed up with the dames,
It's time I got rid of them for good,
And because of that I've made a plan
To wear a frock and become a monk.

Markos Vamvakaris, c. 1940. *Courtesy of the Gennadius Library.*

Sotiria Bellou, Tomboys & Lesbianism in Rebetika

Sotiria Bellou (1921-1997) was one of Greece's most celebrated singers of rebetiko and laiko song. Much loved in Greece and in the diaspora the world over, she is one of rebetika's queer trailblazers, being openly gay in a time when such a thing was unheard of. Gail Holst characterises her as thus:

> "One of the most remarkable performers of rebetika...Nothing about her life or personality conformed to Greek norms of female behaviour...For one thing she was a remarkable singer; for another she was openly gay. Neither her gender nor her sexual preferences seem to have stood in the way of her career..." (Holst, 2003: 175-176)

Thankfully, an American academic is conducting pioneering research into Bellou's sexual and gender identity, along with the discourses surrounding it. This will eventually take the form of a critical biography, with an approach that "will demonstrate the significance of Bellou to non-Greeks, and will return her to her fellow Greeks anew." (Dixon, 2018: 4)

According to Nina Rapi, Bellou was a "lesbian icon" who "donned a classic butch image of slicked back hair, dark glasses, and *mangia* for decades."

It is surprising that even though rebetika has long been associated with American blues music, that there hasn't been much comparison between queer blues-women like Ma Rainey, Bessie Smith and Billie Holiday, and their rebetika counterparts.

When I was in Athens in late-2018, a friend passed on a rumour from a well-known collector and researcher, that the rebetiko/laiko singer and lyricist Ioanna Georgakopoulou (1920-2007) was bisexual. Although I neither read nor heard of any other information on her rumoured lesbian sexuality, this piece of hearsay prompted me to look closely at Georgakopoulou's recorded repertoire as a singer, as well as the 46 songs that are credited to her as a composer (see bibliography: Rebetiko Sealabs, 2019).

Bellou the "lesbian icon", photo c. 1940s.

Bellou singing at a concert/exhibition on rebetika organised by Petropoulos at the Athens Hilton on 9-5-1968.
Courtesy Gennadius Library, Elias Petropoulos papers.

Georgakopoulou (middle) with microphone stand in Thessaloniki in 1948. *Courtesy Gennadius Library, Elias Petropoulos papers.*

Georgakopoulou, in the documentary Νυχτερινός Επίσκεπτης (1994). She seems to have adopted a more androgynous look from the 1970s onwards.

Georgakopoulou was born in the city of Pyrgos in 1920 and moved to Athens after her father died when she was two years old. From the age of eight she sang in the local parish choir and was later discovered by a singer of *elafro*, or light-popular song, who helped organise her recording debut. Issued in 1938, her first record featured the songs "Christina" and "My Smyrnan Girl" [Σμυρνιά Μου]; the latter with lyrics written by Kostas Kofiniotis. Georgakopoulou sings:

> When you come onto your balcony,
> My flirty Smyrnan girl.
>
> You do it to me and I go crazy,
> From all of this yearning.
>
> You are sweet like sherbet,
> White like cream.
>
> And for both of those eyes
> I roam the streets tortured.

It is currently unclear whether the 46 songs credited under her name were actually composed by her, although some sources concede that she at least wrote the lyrics, with the music created by one of her collaborators, either Tsitsanis or Mitsakis.

Looking at this pool of 46 songs alone – and disregarding other songs she sang on record but wasn't credited for – some clear themes emerge. Unrequited love, pained love, separation, orientalist fantasies, yearning and desire for women, and female characters in general, all feature prominently. Take for example, the song with the most provocative title: "You are the woman I crave" (1948) [Είσαι η γυναίκα που γουστάρω]. Georgakopoulou sings in the first verse:

> You are the woman I crave, come here so I can have you,
> I yearn for you and that's why I say it, I can't endure it any
> longer. Cause you're the woman I crave.

In the song "For you I get drunk every night" (1948) [Για σε μεθώ κάθε βραδιά] she sings:

> One night we lived together,
> But my mind always relives it.
> You were a dream in the dark,
> A masteress of caresses,
> And you left me hopelessly wounded.
>
> You were so attractive,
> An anonymous fling.
> I sweetly danced beside you,
> And I didn't even know your name
> But my heart will always desire you.

In another song credited under her name: "Sweet Fairies" (1947) [Γλυκιές νεράιδες], she sings of:

> Sweet fairies, and sweet girls
> On far away seashores.

Other orientalist-type songs she wrote and sang featuring exotic women and locales are: "Brazilian Woman" (1948), "Argentine Woman" (1947), "The Sudanese" (1947), "The Curse of the Gypsy Woman" (1948), "Allah's Cursed Woman" (1948) and "Nights in Hawaii" (1947).

It must be noted that while Georgakopoulou is usually accompanied by other singers on these recordings, she always takes the lead voice. When she confidently proclaims lines like "you are the woman I crave", foremost as a singer who identified and was acknowledged as a woman – and regardless if she actually wrote the lyrics or not - it is hard not to speculate.

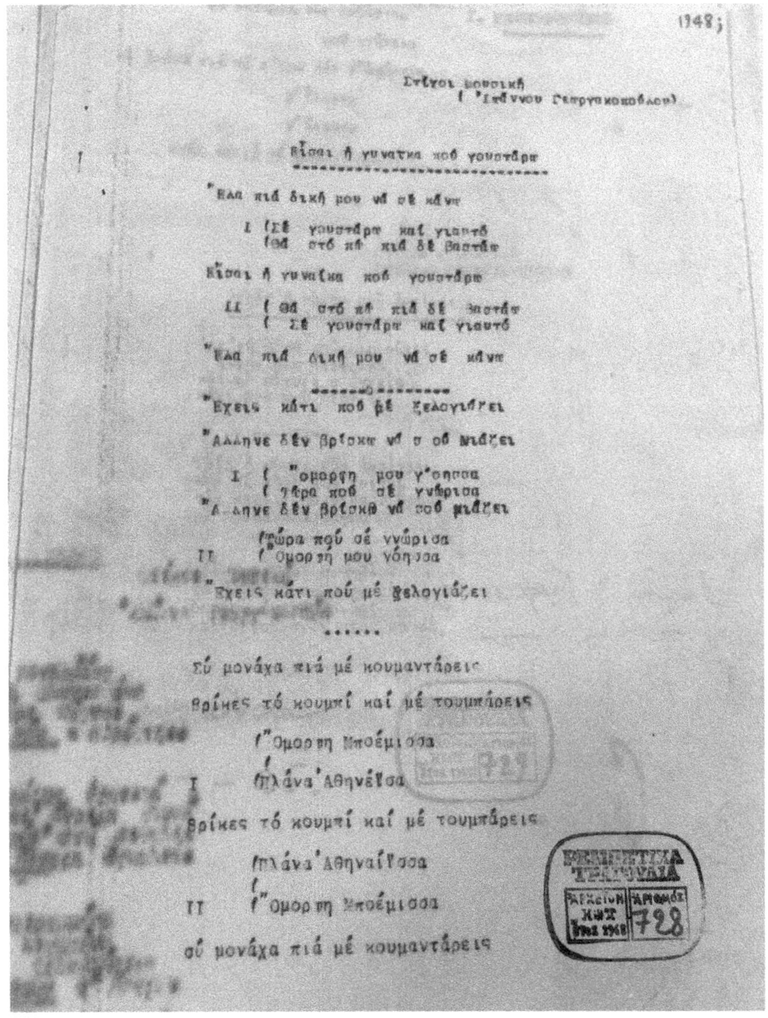

Type-written lyric sheet for Georgakopoulou's song "You are the woman I crave" (1948). *Courtesy Gennadius Library, Elias Petropoulos archives.*

Further on the topic of unrecognised Queerbetika singers, an undisclosed informant learnt from the son of famous bouzouki player Jack Halikias (1898-1957), that when the popular singer Rena Dalia visited America in the 1950s she flirted with Hope Xenos, the wife of Halikias Snr.

Rena Dalia (1934-2000)

More intriguing are photos from Petropoulos's photo archive of the rebetiko/laiko singer Anna Hrysafi (1921-2013) donning very "butch" attire. Photos of Hrysafi show her alternating between androgynous and feminine modes of dress and appearance.

Hrysafi in the early 1950s.

(Left-right) Giorgos Zambetas, Hrysafi and Giorgos Mitsakis in a film from 1956. *Photos courtesy Gennadius Library, Elias Petropoulos papers.*

Hrysafi and Giorgos Mitsakis c. mid-1950s. *Courtesy Gennadius Library, Elias Petropoulos papers.*

Hrysafi (2nd from left) with other singers from the 1950s.
The owner of the *magazi* on the far right.

Hrysafi (3rd from left) and Mitsakis (5th from left) c. 1955.
Photos courtesy Gennadius Library, Elias Petropoulos papers.

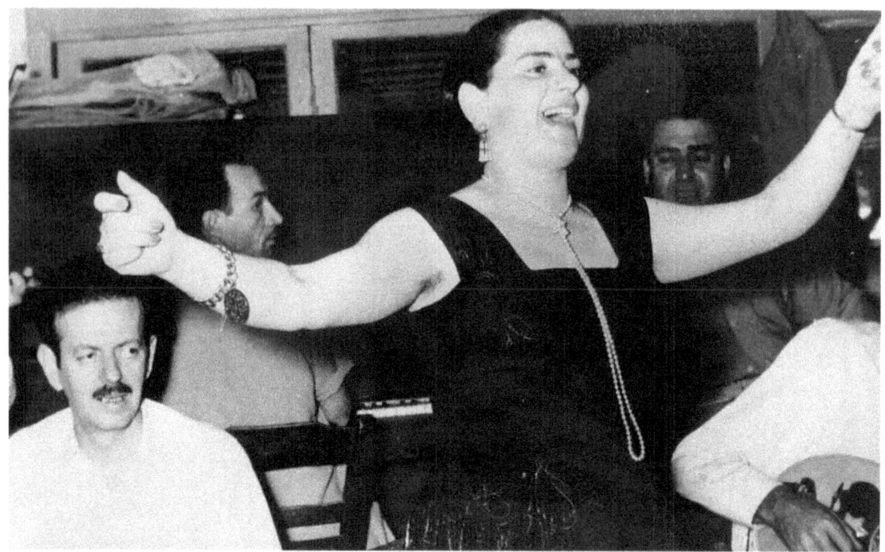

Vassilis Tsitsanis (left) and Hrysafi in 1952. *Courtesy Gennadius Library.*

Hrysafi c. 1950s, with her autograph.
Courtesy Gennadius Library

Hrysafi as pictured on the back of
an LP (1984).

And here, photos of singers Stella Haskil (1918-1954), Hrysafi and Sevas Hanoum (1931-1990).

Haskil c. late 1940s.

Haskil and an unknown woman c. early 1950s.

Hrysafi (right) seeks an autograph from Italian singer Luciano Tajoli. c. 1950s. *Courtesy Gennadius Library, Elias Petropoulos papers.*

Sevas Hanoum at the "Moustaka" with a cigarette in her hand.

And a few extracts from songs that make reference to "tomboys" (see anthology):

<u>Tomboy girl</u> (1929)

Come and heal the wound you've opened,
I ache for you, my tomboy girl,
You took my heart away and left me breathless,
Come on, my gorgeous one.

<u>The Tomboy</u> (1950)

I smoke, I drink, and I make my rounds,
I snub every man I meet.

I hold the cigarette like a lady-gentleman,
that's why they call me the crazy tomboy.

<u>Valentina</u> (1950)

Ah! Valentina! Ah! You crazy flirt!
Your hair is cut short
And you talk like a tomboy.

And the way you're going, in a few years
You'll be wearing pants.
Valentina! Valentina!

Two songs recorded in 1933 also shed light on the theme of lesbian sexuality within the world of rebetiko, with the following characteristic verses (see anthology):

<u>I'm Becoming a Man</u> (1933)

There's no gal like me in all of Athens,
I'm becoming a man, first thing's first, with a pistol and dagger,
I have a whore as my girlfriend, and I've given her my all.

When I head into the hash den, I look at them all sideways
And they say to me, "hey brother, take a drag and have a good time"

<u>If I were a man</u> (1933)

If I were a man, I'd set Piraeus and Athens on fire
they'd call me Vaggo and they wouldn't call me Dina.

I'd have women as my dames, by the week's end I'd have ten
But I curse my mother because she made me a woman.

Ah, wretched world, I curse you for this injustice
Because in my heart I was never born a woman.

2. Sites of Homosociality

a visual essay

"The songs and dances of the rebetika flourished within the almost exclusively male communities of the hashish den, the merchant navy, the prisons, and the dockyards."

(Holst, 2003: 177)

Prisons/Στη Φυλακή

93652

Hash-dens/Στο Τεκέ

‹ΜΕΣ ΤΟΥ ΝΙΚΗΤΑ ΤΟΝ ΝΤΕΚΕ›

Army/Στο Στρατό

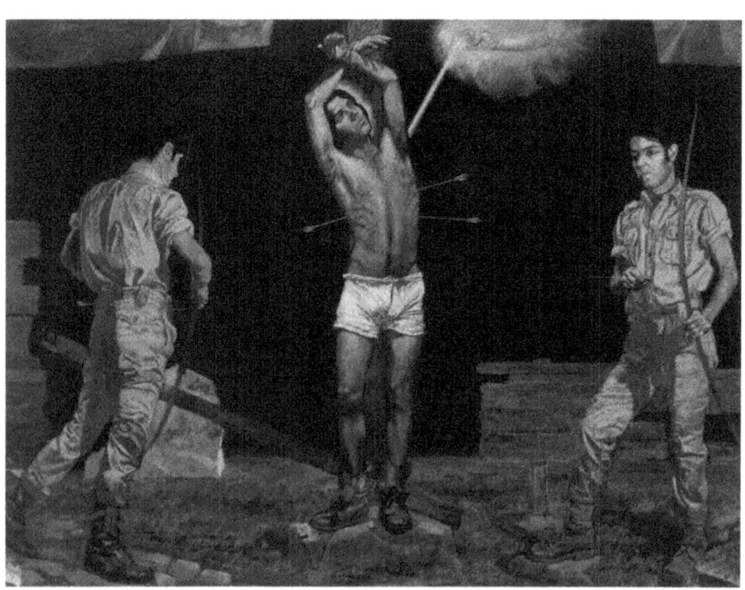

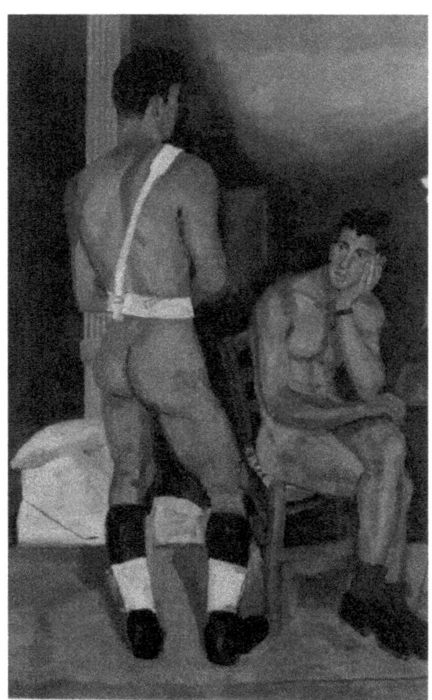

Y.M.C.A
FOR
YOUR
BOY
UNITED WAR WORK CAMPAIGN
NOVEMBER 11-18, 1918

Navy/Ναυτικό

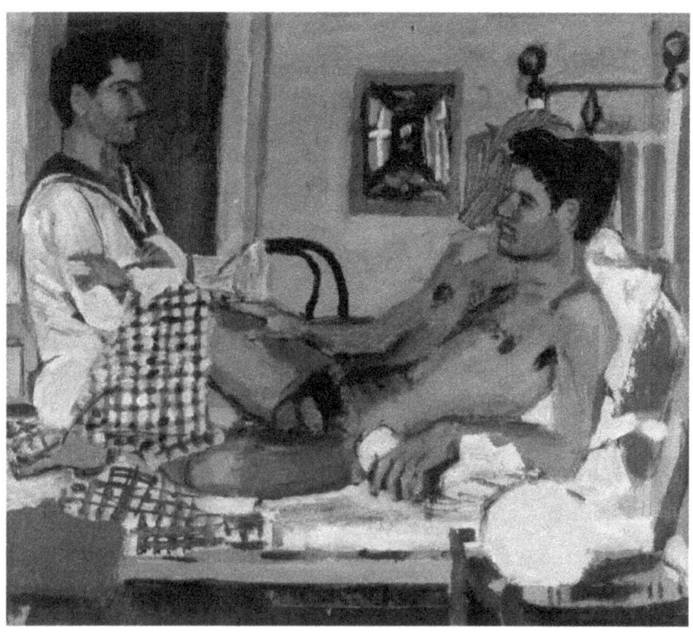

JOIN THE NAVY
THE SERVICE FOR
FIGHTING MEN

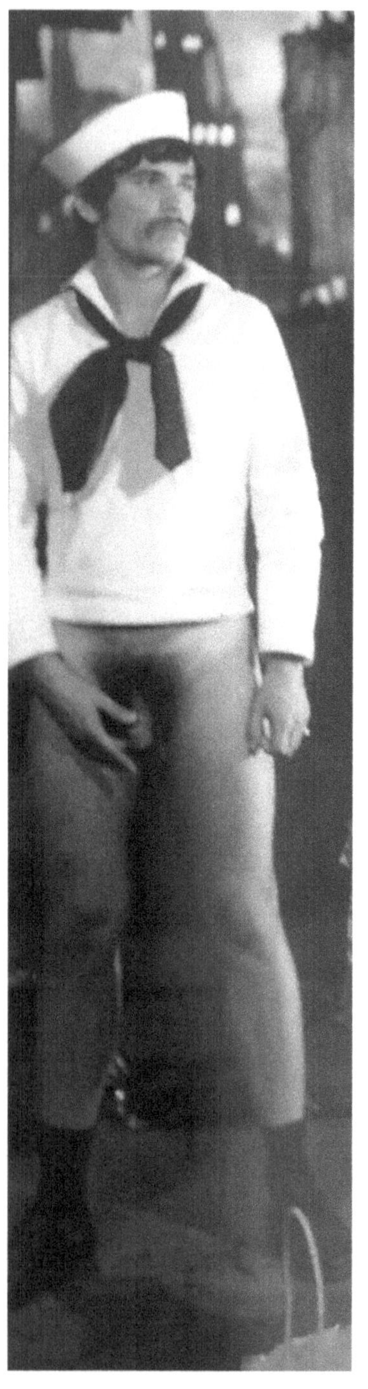

KIAKIΣ

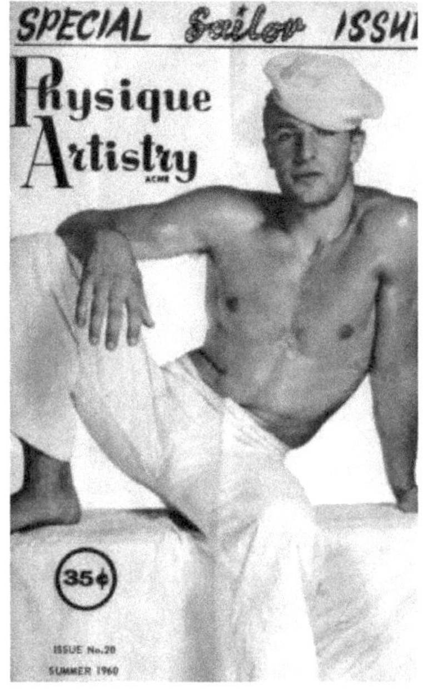
SPECIAL Sailor ISSUE
Physique
Artistry
ACME
35¢
ISSUE No.20
SUMMER 1960

3. Gay Pro-Rebetika Literati

"Re your research topic, it's doubtless occurred to you already that Tsarouchis, Hadjidakis, Christianopoulos and Tachtsis were prominent gay trail-blazers of post-war pro-rebetika discourse. You may also wish to note a prior (inter-war) generation of gay rebetophiles, notably Napoleon Lapathiotis [and] Mitsos Papanikolaou."

- Stathis Gauntlett, email message to the author, 9/12/2018.

Napoleon Lapathiotis (1888 – 1944)

Lapathiotis was a writer and poet, born in Athens on October 31, 1888. He went on to study law at Athens University but never practiced the profession. Despite his middle to upper class background, he seems to have taken an interest in the "low-life" rebetika and the drug culture surrounding it. He was also openly gay, a communist, was addicted to opium, and lived the life of an "aesthete." It is rumoured that he visited the hash dens of Piraeus and met Yiorgos Batis, an influential rebetika musician. Lapathiotis wrote a teke-inspired poem that only came to light years after his death. It starts with the line "Down in Mitsos's hash-den" and includes many slang words. According to Stathis Gauntlett, "it borders on parody in its combination of rebetika themes with formula patterns from historical and lyrical folksongs." (2005: 95)

Κάτω στου Μήτσου το τεκέ κάναν οι μπάτσοι μπλόκο,
Και βρήκαν ντουμανότρυπες κι ένα γιαπί λουλάδες,
Πενηνταδυό διμούτσουνες και δεκαοχτώ μαρκούτσια.
Σουρτά, σουρτά με μπαμπεσιά, ζυγώσαν οι ρουφιάνοι
Με ζούλα ήρθαν οι πούστηδες και μας εβάναν μπροστά:
Τσιμπήσαν πρώτα το Μπαλήν όπου φυλούσε τσίλλιες
Και μπήκαν στο τσαρδάκι μας και μας τα κάναν λίμπα!
Πήραν τις ντουμανότρυπες, πήραν και τους λουλάδες,
Πήραν και τις διμούτσουνες τα δεκαοχτώ μαρκούτσια
Πήραν και τους ντερβίσηδες και στο πλεκτό τους πάνε,
Πήραν το Μίκα το Ντουρντή το τζε του Νταλαβέρη
Το Μπάρμπουλα, το Μπόρμπουλα και το Μπαλή το Μήτσο
Πήρανε και το Ντερτιλή το Ντάτα το θηρίο
Πούκαντε πέντε στη Παλιά και δώδεκα στ' Ανάπλι
Κι όντας τσακίζεται λέει: Οφ, τ' αδερφάκι!
Πήραν και το Σκουντή το Λιά με τα σμιχτά τα φρύδια,
κι ο Λιάκος βαρυγκόμαγε, κι ο Λιάκος βλαστημούσε.
Λιάκο μ' τ' έχεις και θλίβεσαι, τ' έχεις κι αναστενάζεις;
Δεν κλαίω που με τσιμπήσανε και στο πλεχτό με πάνε,
μον' κλαίω που μου τη σκάσανε κι ακόμα είμαι χαρμάνι...
(Diktaois, 1984: 53)

Lapathiotis ended up poor and destitute and took his own life with a revolver on January 7, 1944.

Yannis Tsarouchis (1910 – 1989)

The encyclopedia of GLBTQ culture summarised Tsarouchis as follows:

> "One of the most important twentieth-century Greek painters, Yannis Tsarouchis...is one of a group of Greek artists who helped both portray and define modern Greek identity.
> A deeply sensual painter, much influenced by the French impressionists, Tsarouchis is also a significant gay artist who filled his canvases with homoerotic images of vulnerable men and (to a much lesser extent) strong women." – *Tina Gianoulis.*

Tsarouchis was another prominent champion of rebetika, whose paintings hint at the music's homoerotic possibilities, especially with his focus on soldiers and sailors as subjects. In an iconic painting, Tsarouchis depicts two soldiers dancing the zeibekiko, one clutching his testicles as he does so.

Tsarouchis, on the left, dances with fellow artist Nikos Stefanou (1933-) at the "Belle Hydra Isle" in 1966. Sotiria Bellou and Koulis Skarpelis also sang at that venue around the same time. *Courtesy of the Gennadius Library, Elias Petropoulos papers.*

Manos Hadjidakis (1925 – 1994)

Hadjidakis was a gay Greek composer and music theorist who was a major proponent of the _entechno_ genre, a kind of art-music that emerged in the 1950s and which drew upon folk melodies and rhythms, as well as rebetika.

Hadjidakis is well-known for his 1949 lecture on rebetika, where he recruited Sotiria Bellou and Markos Vamvakaris to perform, and championed a genre that was much-maligned at the time, particularly for its associations with the underworld. According to Gail Holst:

> "The presentation of rebetika to a sophisticated Athenian audence by a man respected as a 'serious' composer marked the beginning of the cultivation of rebetika by a significant group of Greek artists and intellectuals, some of whom, like the painter Tsarouchis, undoubtedly shared Hadjidakis's attraction to the exclusively male environment of the songs."

(Holst, 1998: 123)

Two photos of Hadjidakis with Vassilis Tsitsanis, around 1960.
Courtesy of the Gennadius Library, Elias Petropoulos papers.

Kostas Tachtsis (1927 – 1988)

Kostas Tachtsis, a Greek writer who was born in Thessaloniki in 1927, is best known for his novel "The Third Wedding", first published in 1962, which sold over 100,000 copies and was translated into several languages. He was also openly gay and a *"travesti"* (see glossary). In August 1988 he was murdered in his apartment in Athens, aged 61. He was buried at state expense.

In a written foreword to a record of music by Hadjidakis, Tachtsis writes of the significance of rebetika to his generation, who came of age in the years following the German occupation of Greece in 1945. The appeal of this music to the gay literati of his ilk, regardless of whether they were accepted or not as rebetes is made clear in the following passage:

> "In the era of the Civil war, around the years 1945-48, all of us young people who lived in the major urban centers…found ourselves at a dead-end, something unknown to the generations before or after our own…the horrors of the [German] occupation [of World War II] were still alive in our memories and we wanted to forget it all, we wanted to live, and truly living, at that age, was above all about love and song. But what kind of song?
>
> The tango and the waltz lost all credibility due to the liberation. The songs that were brought along by our so-called "liberators", and which were imitated straight away by our money-grubber composers, were basically the same underpants worn inside-out.
>
> The folk songs were still there, of course. However, our generation couldn't stand them: regardless of our cultural descent and heritage, we were children of the "big city", we didn't know these songs, they didn't express us…And thus, we discovered the rebetika…We only sang them. We didn't dance them, it's the truth. The rebetic dances took on a theatrical character when some of us sacrilegiously performed them, when we weren't, or couldn't even try to be initiated rebetes. However, we sang them."
>
> - December 1974. Later republished in (Petropoulos, 1979: 270)

Dinos Christianopoulos (1931 -)

Christianopoulos was born in Thessaloniki in 1931 and is a poet, literary critic and scholar, dubbed by Yannakopoulos as "one of the prominent representatives of the old generation of Greek homosexual intellectuals" (2016). I tried contacting Christianopoulos in late-2018 to ask him questions about my research but was unsuccessful. Close contacts and publishers all informed me that he is seriously unwell.

***

The homoeroticism of his poetry is amply illustrated in the collection of prose-poems "The Naked Piazza" (1983) [Νεκρή Πιάτσα], including one entitled "To a working-class friend":

> Please don't wear perfume
> I like the odour of your body.
> There's no perfume lovelier than your sweat.
> I want to savour the saltiness of your chest,
> To drink in the fragrance of your armpits,
> To soak myself in the moisture of your loins.
> *(trans in Yannakopoulos, 2016: 177)*

In another poem from the same collection, the narrator is taken on a motorbike ride by his lover around Thessaloniki, ending up at a popular night club, now abandoned and derelict. Here, the narrator's reminiscences of great rebetika singers singing "the most sorrowful songs of love" forms the backdrop for the consummation of homosexual desire:

> "Here, only a few years ago, was the popular late-night club, "The Kalamaki." The bedraggled dance floor was still there, and the stage for all the instruments. Here, Tsitsanis and Markos played, here I saw from the barbed wires Giota Lydia singing the song "Lawlessness."
>
> I thought: only love's passion knows how to rise above all this wreckage. And we laid down on the hot cement, and tried to seek it out with tenderness, there where was once heard the most sorrowful songs of love." (1983: 13)

Christianopoulos in the summer of 1948

4. Anthology

Αγοροκοριτσάρα (1929)

Έλα να μου γιάνεις την πληγή, που μ' άνοιξες
και πονώ για σένα, αγοροκοριτσάρα μου,
πήρες την καρδούλα μου, πνοή δε μ' άφησες,
έλα μπαρμπουνάρα μου.

Έλα και μη θέλεις να χαθώ,
αγοροκόριτσο, για σε θα τρελαθώ,
έλα και μη θέλεις να χαθώ,
αγοροκόριτσο, για σε θα τρελαθώ.

Έλα κοντά μου, στην αγκαλιά μου,
έλα και δώσ' μου το φιλί σου το γλυκό,
ίσως γιατρευτώ, εγώ για σένα λιώνω,
αγοροκοριτσάρα μου, σ' αγάπησα πολύ,
πως να σου το 'πώ βαθειά έχω τον πόνο,
έλα πια και δώς μου το φιλί.

Με το τσιγαράκι που φουμάρεις κάβομαι,
άναψε η καρδιά μου, αγορορίτσάρα μου,
αχ, για τα τσαχπίνικά σου σκέρτσα, χάνομαι,
λιώνω, μπαρμπουνάρα μου.

Έλα και μη θέλεις να χαθώ,
αγοροκόριτσο, για σε θα τρελαθώ,
έλα και μη θέλεις να χαθώ,
αγοροκόριτσο, για σε θα τρελαθώ.

Έλα κοντά μου στην αγκαλιά μου,
έλα και δώσ' μου το φιλί σου το γλυκό,
ίσως γιατρευτώ, εγώ για σένα λιώνω,
αγοροκοριτσάρα μου, σ' αγάπησα πολύ,
πως να σου το 'πώ βαθειά έχω τον πόνο,
έλα πια και δώσ μου το φιλί.

Tomboy girl (1929)

Come and heal the wound you've opened
I ache for you, my tomboy girl,
You took my heart away and left me breathless,
Come on, my gorgeous one.

Come on, wish not my end
I go crazy for you, my tomboy girl.
Come on, wish not my end,
I go crazy for you, my tomboy girl.

Come close in my arms,
Come and give me your sweet kiss
And maybe then I'll heal.
I yearn for you, my tomboy girl, I love you dearly.
How can I tell you? My pain is so deep,
Come here and give me your kiss.

With the cigarette you smoke, I'm set ablaze
Light the fire in my heart, my tomboy girl
Ah, with your flirts and whims, I lose my mind,
I'm yearning for you my gorgeous one.

Come on, wish not my end
I go crazy for you, my tomboy girl
Come on, wish not my end,
I go crazy for you, my tomboy girl.

Come close in my arms,
Come and give me your sweet kiss,
And maybe then I'll heal.
I yearn for you, my tomboy girl, I love you dearly,
How can I tell you? My pain is so deep,
Come here and give me your kiss.

Composed by Panayotis Toundas (1886-1942) and sung on record by Kostas Nouros in Athens and issued on Columbia Αγγλίας 18069 sometime in 1929 (according to Maniatis). The same song was recorded and sung by three other artists during 1929. Translated by Michael Alexandratos.

Το λεξικό του μάγκα (Εσπεράντο) (1930)

«Το εννόησες, λέω μπήκες
και τους **ντιγκιτάνγκ**, Μαρίκες...»

The Mangas's Lexicon (Esperanto) (1930)

"To say 'do you understand', I say 'geddit',
and to say '**fags**' I say 'Marikas'..."

[Extract only. Full recording and lyric transcription available here: "Λεξικό
του μάγκα / Track 20" http://libsearch.teiep.gr/Record/1%2F324 (Accessed
15/4/2019)]

This comic routine was first recorded in 1930 and issued on Parlophon Γερμανίας
B-21559. According to rebetiko.sealabs the lyrics were partly authored by Elias
Kapetanakis from the «επιθεώρηση» or theatre review "Lovitoura" (1929). In this
skit, a mangas recites in song and rhyme the supposedly "slang" equivalents
of Greek vernacular words. In the extract above, the slang equivalent of the
word «εννοήσες» or "understand" is «μπήκες» or "geddit?". Following this, the
slang equivalent of the term «ντιγκι-ντανγκ» literally "ding-dong", referring to
the swaying movements of an effeminate man, is «Μαρίκες» literally "Marikas",
from the Spanish derogatory word for a gay man: maricón. Although not a
rebetiko song, this routine is still connected to the world of rebetiko through the
character of the mangas and his slang. The legendary koutsavakis was another
underworld character portrayed in theatre reviews. This routine was recorded
again in 1931.

Τουμπελέκι Τουμπελέκι (1931)

Η τύχη μου το έριξε να κλέψω ένα σακκάκι
το βάσταγα και τράβαγα για το Μοναστηράκι (x2)
τούμπα-τούμπα το λεγένι, βρε, 'κείνο που 'παμε θα γένει, βρε
τουμπελέκι-τουμπελέκι, βρε, που μας κάνεις το λελέκι

Κατά διαβόλου σύμπτωση, να και τ' αφεντικό του
με τράβαγε και μου 'λεγε, πως ήτανε δικό του (x2)
τουμπελέκι-τουμπελέκι, βρε, που μας κάνεις το λελέκι, βρε
τούμπα-τούμπα το λεγένι, βρε,
που μας κάνεις το λεβέντη

Αχ, η ζωή των Γιάννηδων μες στην απελπισία
πότε στα κρατητήρια και πότε σ' ευτυχία (x2)
τουμπελέκι-τουμπελέκι, βρε, που μας κάνεις το λελέκι, βρε
τούμπα-τούμπα το λεγένι, ωχ,
που μας κάνεις το λεβέντη

Βρε, ποιά κυρία, ποιά κουρέλω, βρε ποια κασόμπρα του συρμού
βρε έναν κόμη σαν **τοιούτο** να τον περάσει γι' αλεπού (x2)
τουμπελέκι-τουμπελέκι, βρε, που μας κάνεις το λελέκι, βρε
τούμπα-τούμπα το λεγένι, βρε,
που μας κάνεις το λεβέντη

Βρε, το κοστούμι που φοράω, βρε σ' ένα φίλο το χρωστάω
μα δεν το δίνω, δεν το δίνω, βρε, μα τον Άγιο Κωνσταντίνο(x2)
τουμπελέκι-τουμπελέκι, βρε, που μας κάνεις το λελέκι, ώχ
τούμπα-τούμπα το λεγένι, βρε, που ότι είπαμε θα γένει

Toumbeleki Toumbeleki (1931)

As luck would have it I happened to steal a jacket
I carried it off and went down to Monastiraki (x2)
toumba toumba the wash-basin, oh, what we said will happen
toumbeleki toumbeleki, oh, how come you play all stuck-up

By some diabolical coincidence along came the owner
caught up with me and said it was his (x2)
toumbeleki toumbeleki, oh, how come you play all stuck-up
toumba toumba the wash-basin, oh,
how come you're playing the young brave

Oh, the desperate lives of pickpockets
sometimes in the clink, sometimes joyful (x2)
toumbeleki toumbeleki, oh, how come you play all stuck-up
toumba toumba the wash-basin, oh,
how come you're playing the young brave

Oh, some lady, some rag-bag, oh some fashionable loose girl
oh, one with hair like a **fag**, trying to be the smart guy (x2)
toumbeleki toumbeleki, oh, how come you play all stuck-up
toumba toumba the wash-basin, oh,
how come you're playing the young brave

Oh, the suit I'm wearing I owe it back to a friend
but I'm not giving it back, by St. Constantine (x2)
toumbeleki toumbeleki, oh, how come you play all stuck-up
toumba toumba the wash-basin, oh, what we said will happen

This song was recorded by K. Kostis [pseudonym for Kostas Bezos (1905-1943)] in Athens on May 22nd, 1931 and issued on Orthophonic S-613. According to Tony Klein: "The lyrics, truly unique for their time, contain both stock rebetiko lines, and language which is often very difficult to interpret…That there are references to prostitution and a clandestine gay world would seem to be incontrovertible." The word denoting "fag" in Greek is «ΤΟΙΟΎΤΟ» literally meaning "one such" or "that one". Greek transcription and English translations by Tony Klein and Dimitris Kourtis. Reproduced from the liner notes to "The Jail's a Fine School - A. Kostis", released by Olvido Records in 2015.

Αν ήμουν άντρας (1933)

Αν ήμουν άντρας θα 'καιγα Πειραία και Αθήνα
και Βάγγο ας με λέγανε κι ας μη με λέγαν Ντίνα (x2)

Θα είχα γυναίκες γκόμενες, την εβδομάδα δέκα
μα βλαστημώ τη μάνα μου, που μ' έκανε γυναίκα. (x2)

Πάντα θε να φερνόμουνα σα φίνι κουτσαβάκι
στο χέρι μου θα κράταγα με φούντα μπεγλεράκι. (x2)

Και θα γυρνούσα με ταξί Πειραία και Αθήνα
στις μπύρες και στα καμπαρέ να την περνάω φίνα. (x2)

Αχ, βρε ντουνιά σε βλαστημώ, γιατ' είμ' αδικημένη
γιατί γυναίκα στην καρδιά δεν είμαι γεννημένη. (x2)

If I were a man (1933)

If I were a man, I'd set Piraeus and Athens on fire
they'd call me Vaggo and they wouldn't call me Dina.

I'd have women as my dames, by the week's end I'd have ten
But I curse my mother because she made me a woman.

I always wanted to show off as a fine young brave
In my hand I'd carry tassels of beads.

And I'd go around Piraeus and Athens in a taxi,
In the beer halls and cabarets, I'd have a fine time.

Ah, wretched world, I curse you for this injustice
Because in my heart I was never born a woman.

Composed by Vaggelis Papazoglou (1896-1943) and sung on record by Katina Homatianou and issued on ODEON Ελλάδος GA-1765 around 1933. Hasaposerviko rhythm. Translation by Michael Alexandratos.

Γίνομαι Άνδρας (1933)

Σαν εμένανε, τσαχπίνα, δεν έχ' άλλη στην Αθήνα,
γίνουμ' άντρας πρώτο πράμα, με πιστόλι και με κάμα
κι έχω γκόμενα μια δούλα, και της τα 'χω πάρει ούλα.

Στον τεκέ όταν θα πάω, όλους τους στραβοκοιτάω
και μου λεν', καλώς τ'αδέρφι, τράβα μια να κάνει κέφι
κι αρχινούνε τα μαγκάκια, γλέντι με μπαγλαμαδάκια.

Μα ένα βράδυ μ' ανθιστήκαν, κι όλοι απάνω μου ριχτήκαν
και μ' αρχίσαν στα σορόπια, με τη γλώσσα τους τη ντόπια
και φωνάζαν με λαχτάρα, αχ, αγοροκοριτσάρα.

-Αχ, γειά σου αγοροκόριτσο, γειά σου!

<u>*I'm Becoming a Man*</u> (1933)

There's no gal like me in all of Athens,
I'm becoming a man, first thing's first, with a pistol and dagger.
I have a whore as my girlfriend, and I've given her my all.

When I head into the hash den, I look at them all sideways
And they say to me, "hey brother, take a drag and have a good time"
And the lads all start up, a party with *baglamades*.

But one night they found me out, and it was all heaped upon me,
And they put me onto the sweet stuff, with their own special talk,
And they shouted with praise, ah, you tomboy!

-*To your health tomboy girl, to your health!*

Composition credited to Panayotis Toundas (1886-1942) and sung on record by
Roza Eskenazi (1895-1980) in 1933, Athens, and issued on Parlophone Ελλάδος
B-21674. Zeibekiko rhythm. Also recorded in 1933 by singer Rita Abadzi (1914-
1969) on Columbia Ελλάδος DG-453. Translation by Michael Alexandratos.

Ο Χασάπης (1934)

Χασάπη μου, με την ποδιά που σαν την δέσεις πίσω
όταν σε δω χασάπη μου τώρα θα ξεψυχήσω
χασάπη μου όταν σε δω τώρα θα ξεψυχήσω

Γυαλίζουν τα θηκάρια σου στη μέση που τα βάνεις
με την ποδιά την κόκκινη εσύ θα με τρελάνεις (2)

-Γεια σου Μάρκο μου γειά σου (φωνή Στράτου Παγιουμτζή)

Αστράφτουν τα μαχαίρια σου λάμπει και το μασάτι
Λάμπουν τα μαύρα μάτια σου μαγκίτη μου χασάπη (2)

Παλεύεις με τα αίματα μα δεν πονεί η καρδιά σου
σε αγαπώ, χασάπη μου, μ' αυτήν την λεβεντιά σου
Χασάπη μου σε αγαπώ, μ' αυτήν την λεβεντιά σου.

The Butcher (1934)

Oh my butcher, with the apron you tie up behind
Every time I see you my butcher, I go crazy
My butcher every time I see you, I go crazy.

Your blades shine in the sheath you put them in
With your red apron, it drives me mad.

-To your health Markos, to your health!

Your knives sparkle, your sharpener shines too,
Your dark eyes shine my fine butcher lad.

You deal with all that blood, but your heart never pains,
I love you, my butcher, with your manly ways.
My butcher I love you, with your manly ways.

Music and lyrics attributed to Markos Vamvakaris, who also sang lead vocals and played bouzouki in this song on Columbia Ελλάδος DG-2063, recorded in 1934 in Athens. Hasapiko rhythm. Translation by Michael Alexandratos.

Τραγιάσκες (1934)

Και οι γκόμενες φορέσανε τραγιάσκες
και στους δρόμους τριγυρνούν και κάνουν τσάρκες.
βλέπεις γκόμινα τραγιάσκα να φοράει
και σαν μαγκίτης αβέρτα περπατάει.

Και οι γκόμενες αντρίκια κουσουμάρουν
και με μάγκες τρέχουνε για να φουμάρουν.
βλέπεις μάγκα μου ντερβίσικα κορίτσια,
με ναζάκια με κολπάκια και καπρίτσια.

Βλέπω μια και μια ώρα την κοιτάζω
και σαν με βλέπει την τραγιάσκα κατεβάζω.
είμαι φέρτε να της πω μωρ' αδερφάκι,
ζούλα πάμε στον τεκέ για τσιμπουκάκι.

-_Γειά σου Μάρκο ντερβίση!_

Δεν μπορώ να καταλάβω φίλοι μάγκες
και οι κυρίες κουσουμάρουν με τραγιάσκες.
τι θα κάνουμε εμείς τα ντερβισάκια,
μας ζυγώνουν και μας πιάνουν τα μεράκια.

Cloth Caps (1934)

And the dames wore men's caps
Roaming the streets, doing their strolls.
You see a dame wearing a cap
And she walks quickly like a tough guy.

And the dames act like men,
And they run to smoke with the tough guys.
My dude, do you see the dervish-girls
With their airs, their tricks and their whims?

I see one and stare at her for an hour,
And when she sees me, I tip my cap.
I'm too far away to tell her, my brother
Let's go secretly to the hash-den to smoke pipes.

-To your health Markos, you dervish!

I can't understand, my dudes
that the ladies too, wear their caps.
What are we to do, us dervish-dudes,
When they come to us and steal our fun?

Composition credited to Markos Vamvakaris, who is also the lead singer on the recording Parlophone Ελλάδος B-21710 in 1933 in Athens. Hasapiko rhythm. Translated by Michael Alexandratos.

Ο Ρεμπέτης (1934)

Ο ρεμπέτης στην ταβέρνα μέρα-νύχτα τριγυρνά, αμάν αμάν
και γλεντά με τη λατέρνα, τον κερνάνε και κερνά, αμάν αμάν

Ο ρεμπέτης είναι μάγκας και παιδί μερακλαντάν, αμάν αμάν
και απέχει (εις) παρασάγγας απ' τ' **αγόρια ντίγκι-ντανγκ**, αμάν αμάν.

-Γειά σου Στελλάκη!

Ο ρεμπέτης το φουμάρει το μαυράκι βερεσέ, αμάν αμάν
καθώς πέφτει το βραδάκι πίσω απ' το Μεντρεσέ, αμάν αμάν.

The Rebetis (1934)

Day and night the rebetis hangs around the taverna, aman aman
And he dances to the laterna, and they shout him drinks, aman aman

The rebetis is a mangas and a fine lad too, aman aman
And he keeps his distance from the **fag boys**, aman aman

-To your health Stellaki!

The rebetis smokes hash without a care, aman aman
When night falls behind Medrese, aman aman

Composition credited to Kostas Roumeliotis. Sung by Stellakis Perpiniadis (1899-1977) and issued on Columbia DG-2036 around 1934. Recorded in Athens. Zeibekiko rhythm. Translation by Michael Alexandratos. Note the term **ντίγκι-ντάνγκ** in the glossary.

Μες' Στην Χασάπικη Αγορά (1947)

Μες στη χασάπικη αγορά ένα χασαπάκι,
με την ελίτσα και τα φρύδια τα σμιχτά,
όταν με βλέπει και περνάω από μπροστά του,
τη μαχαιρίτσα του στο κούτσουρο κτυπά,

Τα μαγουλά του κοκκινίζουν και με σφάζουν,
η ομορφιά του μ'έχει κάνει σαν τρελή,
με γοητεύει, με μαγεύει, με παιδεύει,
τον εσυμπάθησα, μανούλα μου, πολύ.

Έχει ένα μπόι λεβεντιά σαν τη λαμπάδα,
να ξέρεις, μάνα μου, τρελά τον αγαπώ
και όπως πάω, αν δεν τον πάρω, θα χτικιάσω,
γι' αυτόνε, μάνα μου, στη μαύρη γη θα μπω.

In the Meat Market (1947)

The butcher's boy in the marketplace
With the bushy brows and the mole on his face,
When he sees me walk in front of him
He stabs the block with his knife so trim

His cheeks blush red they kill me dead.
His beauty's made me lose my head.
He charms, and he enchants, and he puts me in a daze.
I feel for him Mama – can't bear delays!

He's tall and strong and manly like a lamp he's all ablaze.
You have to know, Mama, that I can't help but love him madly.
The way that I am going I'm afraid will turn out badly.
If I can't have him I shall die. I'll peak and pine away.
Because of him, in blackest earth you'll bury me one day.

Composed by Markos Vamvakaris and sung on record by Stella Haskil (1918-1954) on ODEON Ελλάδος GA-7400 in 1947. Recorded in Athens. Hasapiko rhythm. Lyrics translated by Noonie Minogue in (Vamvakaris, 2015: 266).

Αγοροκόριτσο (1950)

Καπνίζω, πίνω και γυρνώ,
Τους άντρες τους περιφρονώ.

Ωραία κι έξυπνα, τους στραπατσάρω,
Για αυτό με λεν' αγοροκόριτσο τρελό.

Θέλω μπουζούκια να γλεντώ,
Κι όταν, θα 'μπω σε καπηλειό.

Σαν μια αφέντισσα, κρατώ τσιγάρο,
Γι' αυτό με λεν' αγοροκόριτσο τρελό.

Όπως μ' αρέσει, περπατώ,
Τι θα μου 'πουνε, δεν κοιτώ.

Εγώ, στα κέφια μου, δε 'βάζω αφέντη
Και ας με λεν' αγοροκόριτσο τρελό.

Tomboy (1950)

I smoke, I drink, and I make my rounds,
I snub every man I meet.

Nice or smart, I run them all over
that's why they call me the crazy tomboy.

I want bouzoukia to party with
whenever I enter the bar.

I hold the cigarette like a lady-gentleman,
that's why they call me the crazy tomboy.

When it suits me, I go walking,
What will they say to me? I don't care.

In my good moods, I don't put on the "gentleman"
And they still call me the crazy tomboy.

Music and lyrics by Spyros Kalfopoulos (1923-2006). Sung by Soula Kalfopoulos (1926-????) on lead vocals, accompanied by Takis Binis (1923-2005) and Stellakis Perpiniadis (1899-1977). Issued on Odeon Ελλάδος GA-7560 in 1950. Recorded in Athens. Hasapiko rhythm. Translation by Michael Alexandratos. See the entry for «αγοροκόριτσο» in the glossary.

Βαλεντίνα (1950)

Αχ! Βαλεντίνα! Αχ! Βρε τσαχπίνα!
Μόρτικα κομμένα τα μαλλιά σου,
σαν αγοροκόριτσο η μιλιά σου.
Έχεις κούρσα και σωφάρεις
κι όπου θέλεις ρεμιζάρεις,
έγινες και σωφερίνα!

[Κι όπως πας, σε λίγα χρόνια,
θα φορέσεις παντελόνια.
Βαλεντίνα! Βαλεντίνα!] x2

Αχ! Βαλεντίνα! Αχ! Βρε τσαχπίνα!
Είσαι μια μποέμισσα σπουδαία,
κάνεις την πιο όμορφη παρέα!
Στα μπουζούκια σαν πηγαίνεις
και χασάπικο χορεύεις,
ξετρελαίνεις την Αθήνα!

[Κι όλοι οι άντρες σ' αγαπούνε
και παντού σε συζητούνε!
Βαλεντίνα! Βαλεντίνα!] x2

Έχεις κούρσα και σωφάρεις
κι όπου θέλεις ρεμιζάρεις,
έγινες και σωφερίνα!

[Κι όπως πας, σε λίγα χρόνια,
θα φορέσεις παντελόνια.
Βαλεντίνα! Βαλεντίνα!] x2

Valentina (1950)

Ah! Valentina! Ah! You crazy flirt!
Your hair is cut short
And you talk like a tomboy.
You drive a car
And park wherever you want.
You even became a taxi-driver!

And the way you're going, in a few years
You'll be wearing pants.
Valentina! Valentina!

Ah! Valentina! Ah! You crazy flirt!
You're a special kind of woman
And you're the best company too!
You go to the bouzoukia
And dance the *hasapiko*,
You drive all of Athens wild!

All the guys love you
And everywhere they ask for you!
Valentina! Valentina!

You drive a car
And park wherever you want
You even became a taxi-driver!

And the way you're going, in a few years
You'll be wearing pants.
Oh, Valentina! Valentina!

Music and lyrics by Giorgos Mitsakis (1921-1993) and sung by Mitsakis, Marika Ninou (1918-1957) and Yannis Tatasopoulos (1928-2001) on Columbia Ελλάδος DG-6828 in 1950. Recorded in Athens. Hasapo-serviko rhythm. Translation by Michael Alexandratos.

Έλα Όπως Είσαι (1954)

Έλα όπως είσαι, έλα όπως είσαι,
μη μου χαλάς τα γούστα μου και τη φωτιά μου σβήσε!
Την κούρσα σού 'χω αγκαζέ, μ' όλα τα μεγαλεία,
θυμάρι, θέλεις, κούκλα μου ή μήπως παραλία;

Έλα, μάνα μου, όπως είσαι,
έλα, όπως είσαι!

Η νύχτα είναι δική μας, η νύχτα είναι δική μας
και πρέπει να γλεντήσουμε με όλη την ψυχή μας.
Στα κέφια πάνω, κούκλα μου, θα κάνουμε στραπάτσα,
για γούστο θα το κάψουμε, λεφτά υπάρχουν μάτσα!

Έλα, μάνα μου, όπως είσαι,
έλα, όπως είσαι!

Μες την αγκαλιά σου, μες την αγκαλιά σου,
με ζάλισαν τα χάδια σου, με κάψαν τα φιλιά σου!
Όπου κι αν σε περπάτησα, φωνάξαν "Μπράβο, μάγκα!"
"Κι η κοπελάρα που γλεντάς, πολλά αξίζει φράγκα!"

Έλα, μάνα μου, όπως είσαι,
έλα, όπως είσαι!

Come As You Are (1954)

Come as you are, come as you are,
Don't ruin my fun and dampen my fire!
In your car we were arm in arm, having such a time,
Babe, do you want to go to the beach, or have some grass?

Come on, mama,
Come as you are!

The night is ours, the night is ours,
And we must party with all of our soul
With joy all around we'll bring this place down,
For fun we'll burn it all up, there's plenty of money to blow!

Come on, mama,
Come as you are!

In your embrace, in your embrace,
Your caresses drove me mad, your kisses burned me up!
Wherever I walked with you, they shouted "Bravo lad!"
"And the gal you party with looks a million!"

Come on, mama,
Come as you are!

Music and lyrics credited to Vassilis Tsitsanis (1915-1984) and sung on record by Tsitsanis and Marika Ninou (1918-1957). Recorded in Athens on 10/02/1954 and issued on Odeon GA 7765. Zeibekiko rhythm. This song makes no references to queer gender or sexuality and was chosen simply because some verses express sentiments that are evoked in contemporary discourses surrounding LGBTQI rights and anti-discrimination, e.g. "Come as you are." If we take these sentiments further, we can re-imagine this phrase as one that signals the acceptance and acknowledgement of all the "peripheral" or "othered" people who contributed to the world of rebetiko, including refugees, the working class, sex workers, drug addicts, women and queers.

<u>*Από Την Πόλη Έρχομαι*</u> (c. 1960s)

Το βλέπεις κείνο το βουνό όπου 'ναι ένα κεράσι;
Ο πούτσος μου στον κώλο σου κοντεύει να γεράσει.

Άπο την Πόλη έρχομαι, κρατώντας το βιολί μου,
Καθάρισε τον κώλο σου να βάλω το καυλί μου.

From the "City" I Come (c. 1960s)

Do you see that mountain where there's a cherry tree?
My dick up your ass is getting old.

From the "City" I come, carrying my violin,
Clean up your ass so I can stick my prick in.

These two verses were first published by Elias Petropoulos in the second-edition of his Rebetika anthology in 1979 under the category of "prison songs." He designates the verses as an "old prison *mourmouriko*" and that they were collected by Stathis Gauntlett. The first verse is a lewd parody of a folk song titled «Το βλέπεις εκείνο το βουνό» [Do you see that mountain over there]. The second verse is another lewd parody of a folk proverb «Από την πόλη έρχομαι και στην κορφή κανέλα» [From the "City" I come and from the cinnamon tops]. The "City" here refers to Constantinople, or modern-day Istanbul. Mary Koukoules has anthologised similar obscene parodies in her volumes of Modern Greek erotic folklore and profanities.

However, Petropoulos's designation of this material as an "old prison mourmouriko" is completely spurious. Gauntlett informed me via email correspondence (9/12/2018) that in 1972 he was "asked by a family friend in Athens to pass on those verses to Elias for his archive of Kaliarda-related matter [on Greek gay slang]", and not for his rebetika anthology. He told Petropoulos that his friend had seen them written on a toilet door during his military service in the 1960s. The final directive "clean up your ass" therefore makes sense in this context. This example brings into serious doubt the assigned provenance of other verses in Petropoulos's anthology of "non-commercial rebetika."
Translation by Michael Alexandratos.

Πούστης τον πούστη... (1968)

Πούστης τον πούστη αγαπά, πουτάνα την πουτάνα,
κι ο Γιώργης ο κολομπαράς τους παίρνει όλους σβάρνα.

Fag Loves A Fag... (1968)

Fag loves a fag, slut loves a slut,
but Yiorgos the stag will hunt any butt.

These lyrics were first published in Elias Petropoulos's book "Rebetika Songs" in 1968. They are anthologised under the category "songs of the underworld" on pg 226 of the first-edition and are described as being a fragment of a *zeibekiko* song of unknown authorship, and tentatively dated to 1915. In the second-edition of Petropoulos's anthology in 1979, this date is removed and instead the verse is described as a fragment of an "old *mourmouriko*" song. Petropoulos still notes the song as a zeibekiko but also writes that "today it lives on as a prison proverb" and that "instead of Yiorgos, other names can be substituted, like Kostas." Also note the word «κολομπαράς» in the glossary, translated here as "stag". Regardless of the exact provenance of this verse, it neatly illustrates the similar social standing of 'passive' homosexuals and female prostitutes within the urban milieu, as compared to the masculine "*kolobaras*", who assumes literal and metaphorical power over both by assuming the "top" or active role in hetero or homosex, and who is not stigmatised as a result. This English translation is by John Taylor and is reproduced from an abridged 1992 edition of Petropoulos's rebetika anthology.

Κούνα, Μπέμπη (1973)

Κούνα, μπέμπη, τον κεφτέ σου
Να φχαριστηθεί ο τζές σου.

Κούνα, μπέμπη, τον κλανιά σου
Να φχαριστηθεί η καρδιά σου.

Swing, Baby (1973)

Swing your butt, baby,
To please your lover.

Shake your farter, baby
To please your heart.

These verses were collected by Elias Petropoulos from prisoner and hash-dealer Kostas Andonakos on 17/7/1973, according to a March 2000 article titled «Ο μυστήρος Σακαφλιάς». In the article, Petropoulos does not specify the exact origin of these verses, stating only that Andonakos sang him "old *mourmourika* songs from the hash-dens". They were first published and translated by Katherine Butterworth and Sara Schneider in their 1975 book on rebetika, where it is described as "an old unpublished song from the jails. It is the only homosexual song that has surfaced."

The Greek lyrics were published again in the second-edition to Petropoulos's "Rebetika Songs" in 1979, where it is anthologised under the category of "prison songs" and is spuriously dated to 1900. I have therefore dated these lyrics to the year they were first collected (1973). According to Petropoulos the word «τζές» in this context means a "top" or "active" homosexual lover. There were apparently more verses to this song (Petropoulos, 1979: 143).

Γεράματα ρε φίλε μου (1975)

Γεράματα, ρε Γιάννη μου
καθόμουν σε μιαν άκρη
και κοίταγα το πούτσο μου
και μου `φυγε ένα δάκρυ

Πούτσα μου πώς κατάντησες
εσύ σ' αυτό το χάλι
που όταν έβλεπες μουνί
γινόσουνα ατσάλι;

Εθέριεβες, εθύμωνες
γινόσουν άνω κάτω
και γιάτρευες της κάθε μιάς
το μούνο και το πάτο

Πούτσα μου πώς κατάντησες
εσύ σ' αυτό το χάλι
που όταν έβλεπες μουνί
γινόσουνα ατσάλι;

Τώρα κρυμμένος στο βρακί
δε μου ζητάς παιχνίδια
κάθεσαι κι αναπαύεσαι
στα ένδοξα σου αρχίδια

Πούτσα μου πώς κατάντησες
εσύ σ' αυτό το χάλι
που όταν έβλεπες μουνί
γινόσουνα ατσάλι;

Getting old my friend (1975)

I'm getting old, my friend,
I sat to the side
and looked at my dick
and shed a tear.

My dick, how did it get to this,
With you in such a state,
When wherever you saw a cunt
You became hard like steel?

You shot up, you raged,
You were all over the place,
and every time you satisfied
the cunt and the asshole.

My dick, how did it get to this,
With you in such a state,
When wherever you saw a cunt
You became hard like steel?

Now you're hidden in my pants
And you're not asking for fun,
you just sit back and relax
on your illustrious balls.

My dick, how did it get to this,
With you in such a state,
When wherever you saw a cunt
You became hard like steel?

An unpublished song by Stelios Keromitis (1903-1979). Recorded on tape between 1975-1978, with Keromitis singing and playing bouzouki and his friend Yannis Stamoulis aka "Bir Allach" accompanying on guitar. From the collection of Stavros Kourousis.

5. Addenda

Glossary

αγοροκόριτσο, το. (*agorokoritso*) = From the words αγόρι + κορίτσι, literally "boy-girl", a tomboy. Can mean a girl who always socialises with boys, and who behaves and looks like a boy, or simply a lesbian.

αδελφή, η. (*adelfi*) = literally "sister". Similar meaning to the English words fag, faggot, queer or homosexual.

κίναιδος, ο. (*kinaidos* – pl. *kinaidi*) = an effeminate gay man, also a gay man who takes on the passive role in homosex, i.e. a "bottom".

κολομπαράς, ο. (*kolobaras* – pl. *kolobarades*) = From the Turkish *kulambara*. It refers to a gay man who is a "top" and takes on the masculine, active role in homosex. It can also refer to a pederast who favours young boys or men, again taking the "active" role, that of the *erastis*.

κουτσαβάκης, ο. (*koutsavakis* – pl. *koutsavakides*) = a tough, knife-carrying type from the underworld who spoke a particular slang.

λεσβία, η. (*lesvia*) = lesbian.

μάγκας, ο. (*mangas* – pl. *manges*) = a word that requires a page length's exegesis. Very simply it refers to a kind of man who embodied the ideals of "*mangia*", a way of life to be found in the underworld cities and ports of 19th-20th century Greece, strongly associated with toughness, honour, bravery, manliness and criminality.

μπινές, ο, (*bines* – pl. *binedes*) = from the Turkish ibne, can mean "bisexual", or a male who takes on both passive and active roles in sex, i.e. "versatile".

ντίγκι-ντάνγκας, ο. (*digi-dangas*) = literally "ding-dong" and likely of onomatopoeic origin, referring to the swaying movements of an effeminate gay man. Meaning gay, homosexual, queer, fag, faggot etc.

124

ντιντής, o, (*didis*) = from the nickname for Constantine (**Ντιντής**). It can mean a well-mannered man from high society, who is well-bred and well-kept in his appearance and looks, who is not necessarily a homosexual. It is the antonym of the *mangas* or working-class man. When used as a slang term it can also take on an ironic or derogatory meaning and refer to someone who is gay or effeminate.

πούστης, o. (*poustis* – pl. *poustides*) = gay, fag, faggot, homosexual, queer, although it does not always have a derogatory meaning and can be a playful form of address or endearment between friends and lovers.

πουστόμαγκας, o. (*poustomangas* – pl. *poustomanges*) = "gay-mangas", "faggot-mangas" or "queer-mangas", although tough and masculine in behaviour and appearance, not effeminate. A combination of the words *poustis* + *mangas*.

ρεμπέτης, o. (*rebetis* – pl. *rebetes*) = in short, a free-spirited type who embodied the bohemian life of the subculture that produced rebetiko.

τζές, o. (*tzes*) = slang term for an attractive man who draws attention from and is interested in women or gay men. Can also mean lover, boyfriend or sweetheart.

τιούτος, o. (*tioutos*) = literally "one such", "that way" or "that one", meaning a homosexual.

τραβεστί, o, η. (*travesti*) = From the French: "travesti". Refers to male homosexuals who imitate women in their dress and mannerisms. It is equivalent to the term "transvestite" in English.

ψυχοπαπάς, o. (*psychopapas*) = a *mangiko* slang term for a gay pimp. First published in the glossary to Petros Pikros's novel "Toumbeki…" (1927). Petropoulos also re-published the term in his 1968 rebetic glossary.

Sources used: slang.gr - glossary in (Vamvakaris, 2015: xi-xiv) - (Petropoulos, 1971). Λέξικο της λαϊκής και της περιθωριακής μας γλώσσας - Γιώργος Β. Κάτος, Θεσσαλονίκη, 2016.

Bibliography

Apostolidou, Anna. 2017. "Greek nationhood and 'Greek love': sexualizing the nation and multiple readings of the glorious Greek past". In *Nations and Nationalism*. pp. 68-86.

Barker, Meg-John, and Julia Scheele. 2016. *Queer: A Graphic History*. Icon Books.

Butterworth, Catherine and Sarah Schneider, editors. 1975. *Rebetika: Songs from the Old Greek Underworld*. Athens.

Christianopoulos, Dinos. 1983. Νεκρή Πιάτσα [The Naked Piazza]. Thessaloniki.

------------------------. 1986. Οι Ρεμπέτες του Ντουνιά [The Rebetes of this World]. Thessaloniki.

Davis, Angela. 1999. *Blues Legacies and Black Feminism: Gertrude "Ma" Rainey, Bessie Smith, And Billie Holiday*. New York.

Diktaios, Aris. 1984. Ναπολέων Λαπαθιώτης (Η Ζωή Του – Το Έργο Του) [Napoleon Lapathiotis (His Life – His Work)]. Athens.

Dixon, Kathleen. 2018. Sotiria Bellou, *Her "Backward Self: A Prolegomenon*. Athens.

Gauntlett, Stathis. 2005. "The sub-canonical meets the non-canonical: rebetika and inter-war Greek literature." In *Κάμπος: Cambridge Papers in Modern Greek*, No. 13.

------------------------. 2019. "Rebetika, The Blues of Greece - And Australia." In *Greek Music In America*. edited by Tina Bucuvalas, University Press of Mississippi, Jackson, pp. 105-118.

Herring, Scott. 2007. *Queering The Underworld: Slumming, Literature, And The Undoing Of Lesbian And Gay History*. University of Chicago Press.

Holst-Warhaft, Gail. 1975. *Road to Rembetika*. Athens.

------------------------. 1998. "Rebetika: The Double-descended Deep Songs of Greece." In *The Passion of Music and Dance: Body, Gender and Sexuality*. pp. 111-126. Oxford.

------------------------. 2000. "Amanes: The Legacy Of The Oriental Mother." In *Greek Music In America*. edited by Tina Bucuvalas, University Press Of Mississippi, 2019, pp. 87-104. First published 2000.

------------------------. 2003. "The Female Dervish and Other Shady Ladies of the Rebetika." In *Music and Gender: Perspectives from the Mediterranean*. edited by Tullia Magrini. pp. 169-194. University of Chicago Press,

Koglin, Daniel. 2016. *Greek rebetiko from a psychocultural perspective: Same songs changing minds*. Surrey, England.

Koukoules, Mary. 1983. *Loose-Tongued Greeks: A Miscellany of Neo-Hellenic Erotic Folklore*. Translated by John Taylor. Paris.

Kounadis, Panayotis. 1993. Liner notes to *Konstantinos Nouros: The Phenomenal Voice from Smyrna*. Falireas CD no. 0430. Athens.

Kumbier, Alana. 2014. *Ephemeral Material: Queering the archive*. Sacramento.

Ladopoulos, Kostas. 2008. "Μαρτυρία γιά το Νούρο - "στοιχείο"; (Nouros)". *http://elkibra-nouros.blogspot.com*. June 15, 2008. (Accessed 25/3/2019).

Magrini, Tullia (ed.). 2003. *Music and Gender: Perspectives from The Mediterranean*. Chicago.

Maniatis, Dionysis. 2006. Η εκ περάτων δισκογραφία γραμμοφώνου: έργα λαϊκών μας καλλιτεχνών [gramophone record discography]. Athens.

Maragidou, Melpomeni. 2017. "Η Ζωή και το Έργο του Ρεμπέτη Κώστα Νούρου, που Γούσταρε Γυναίκες και Άνδρες [The Life and Work of the Rebetis Kostas Nouros, who was into Women and Men]". *https:// www.vice.com/gr/article/a3zeb4/h-zwh-kai-to-ergo-toy-rempeth-kwsta-noyroy-poy-goystare-gynaikes-kai-andres.* Vice. June 8, 2017. (Accessed 20/3/2019).

Morris, Roderick Conway. 1981. "Greek Café Music." In *Greek Music in America.* ed. by Tina Bucuvalas, University Press of Mississippi, Jackson, 2019, pp. 71-86. First published, 1981.

Papanikolaou, Dimitris. 2014. "Mapping/Unmapping: The making of queer Athens". In *Queer Cities, Queer Cultures: Europe Since 1945.* pp. 151-170. London.

Petropoulos, Elias. 1968. Ρεμπέτικα Τραγούδια: Λαογραφική έρευνα [Rebetika Songs: A Folkloric Study]. Athens. First edition 1968. Expanded second edition of 1979 and final 1991 edition also consulted.

-----------------------. 1980. Καλιαρντά [Kaliarda]. Athens. First published in 1971.
-----------------------. 1980. Υπόκοσμος και καραγκιόζης [Underworld and Shadow Theatre]. Athens.
-----------------------. 1990. Ρεμπετολογία [Rebetology]. Athens.
-----------------------. 1991. Το Άγιο Χασισάκι [Holy Hashish]. Athens.
-----------------------. 2000. *Songs of the Greek Underworld: The Rebetika Tradition,* trans. Ed Emery. London.
-----------------------. 2001. Καπανταήδες και μαχαιροβγάλτες [Knives and Pistols]. Athens.

Pisimisis, Vasilis. 2010. Βούρλα-Τρούμπα: Περιήγηση στο χώρο του υποκόσμου και της πορνείας του Πειραιά (1840-1968) [Vourla-Trouba: a tour of the underworld and prostitution areas of Piraeus (1840-1968)]. Athens.

Rebetiko Sealabs. 2019 (????). "Η Ιωάννα Γεωργακοπούλου σε τραγούδια που φέρονται ως συνθέσεις της [Ioanna Georgakopoulou in songs which are credited as her compositions]."

rebetiko.sealabs.net/mediawiki/index.php/Η_Ιωάννα_Γεοργακοπούλου_ σε_τραγούδια_που_φέρονται_ως_συνθέσεις_της. (Accessed 10/4/2019)

Sandouri Dean Bey. 2006. "Rembetiko of the Month - June." *Aman Yala.* *http://amanyala.blogspot.com/2006/06/rembetiko-of-month.html.* June 20, 2006. (Accessed 20/1/2019).

Shay, Anthony and Barbara Sellers-Young (ed.). 2005. *Belly Dance: Orientalism, Transnationalism and Harem Fantasy.* California.

Sontag, Susan. 1977. *On Photography.* Penguin Books.

Spyriadou, Konstantia. 2014. Η Κοινωνική Θέση των Γυναικών στα Ρεμπέτικα Τραγούδια του Ελληνικού Μεσοπολέμου (1922 – 1940) [The Social Place of Women in Rebetika Songs of the Greek inter-war years (1922-1940)]. Thessaloniki.

Vamvakaris, Markos. 2015. Αυτοβιογραφία [Autobiography]. Edited by Angeliki Vellou Keil. Athens. First published 1978 in Greek. English edition translated and edited by Noonie Minogue (2015).

Vlisidis, Kostas (ed.). 2018. Σπάνια κείμενα για το ρεμπέτικο (1929-1959) [Rare texts on the rebetiko]. Athens, 2nd expanded edition.

Washabaugh, William (ed.). 1998. *The Passion of Music and Dance: Body, Gender and Sexuality.* Oxford.

Yannakopoulos, Kostas. 2016. "Naked Piazza: Male (Homo)Sexualities, Masculinities and Consumer Cultures in Greece Since the 1960s." In *Consumption and gender in Southern Europe since the long 1960s.* ed. Kostis Kornetis et al. pp. 173-189. London.

Zaimakis, Yiannis. 1999. *'Katagogia Akmazonta': Pareklisi kai politismiki dimiourgia, ston Lakko Herakliou (1900-1940).* Athens. First edition: 1999.

***

Acknowledgements

I would firstly like to thank the staff at the Gennadius Library in Athens, Greece, where I undertook archival research in late-2018 using the the papers of Elias Petropoulos. Particular thanks to Dr. Eleftheria Daleziou.

Secondly, I would like to thank Kostas Ladopoulos for our illuminating conversations on all things rebetika and for welcoming me into his home.

I also had the kind support and encouragement of Kathleen Dixon via our lengthy email correspondences.

Charles Howard also gifted me a CD of superb transfers of recordings featuring the great singer Kostas Nouros, for which I am forever grateful.

Numerous insights, anecdotes and info were also proffered by the great rebetika scholar Stathis Gauntlett, as well as Gail Holst-Warhaft.

Brief conversations regarding this topic with Mary Koukoules were also helpful, and illuminating discussions were also had with Aydin Chaloupka, Christos Fanaritis and Bobby Damore.

And finally a massive thank you to Jeremy Zafiropoulos, whose university library card was well-utilised during the research and writing of this zine.